Doctors Under the Stars

Finding adventure—and love—beneath the glittering Antarctic sky

It's the chance of a lifetime to work in the Antarctic, and a chance for each intrepid doctor to escape their painful past. Yet trapped together in the beauty—and danger—of the frozen landscape, colleagues get close, secrets slip out, and tension and passions hit an all-time high!

Find out more in

His Surgeon Under the Southern Lights
by Robin Gianna

Marine biologist Dr. Zeke Edwards and surgeon Dr. Jordan Flynn are not looking for love, but passion leads to a temporary fling. Only, soon they are breaking all their self-imposed rules.

Reunited in the Snow
by Amalie Berlin

Dr. Lia Monterrosa has come to confront the man who left her at the altar—not fall for Dr. Weston MacIntyre all over again! But working so closely together, their rekindled desire is impossible to ignore.

Both available now!

Dear Reader,

When I was asked if I wanted to do a duet with the fabulous Amalie Berlin, I jumped at the chance! Not only is she an awesome writer and a joy to spend time with, she and I are lucky to live in the same state in the US and could actually meet in person to brainstorm. Amalie came up with the idea of the stories being set in a science station in Antarctica, and the research about all that has been fascinating!

Zeke Edwards is a scientist whose work is extremely important to him, partly because of a tragedy in his past. A tragedy that has convinced him he's a man who shouldn't be relied on except when it comes to his work. Surgeon Jordan Flynn is wary of traveling-scientist types after her ex turned out to be a jerk, and has no interest in repeating that mistake with Zeke.

Except spending time working closely together in the Antarctic cold challenges those convictions. Will they learn to trust themselves, and each other?

Robin xoxo

HIS SURGEON UNDER THE SOUTHERN LIGHTS

ROBIN GIANNA

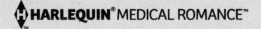

Recycling programs
for this product may
not exist in your area.

ISBN-13: 978-1-335-64185-4

His Surgeon Under the Southern Lights

First North American Publication 2019

Copyright © 2019 by Robin Gianakopoulos

Printed in U.S.A.

Books by Robin Gianna

Harlequin Medical Romance

Christmas in Manhattan
The Spanish Duke's Holiday Proposal
Royal Spring Babies
Baby Surprise for the Doctor Prince
The Hollywood Hills Clinic
The Prince and the Midwife
Midwives On-Call at Christmas
Her Christmas Baby Bump

Flirting with Dr. Off-Limits
It Happened in Paris…
Her Greek Doctor's Proposal
Reunited with His Runaway Bride
Tempted by the Brooding Surgeon
The Family They've Longed For

Visit the Author Profile page
at Harlequin.com for more titles.

To Amalie Berlin—what a privilege to get to write book one of a duet with you. There's no one better in the world to brainstorm with, talk with and laugh with, and I've never drunk so much tea in my life. Let's do it again some time. xoxo

Researching Antarctica has been a fascinating experience, and I'd like to note two resources I particularly enjoyed and appreciated. Thanks to both authors for such interesting and informative reads.

Lost Antarctica: Adventures in a Disappearing Land
by James McClintock

Antarctica: A Year at the Bottom of the World
by Jim Mastro

**Praise for
Robin Gianna**

"The story captures your attention from page one with beautiful prose and a captivating heroine who you instantly fall in love with."
—*Goodreads* on *Baby Surprise for the Doctor Prince*

CHAPTER ONE

WITH THE SHIP pitching from side to side and up and down like a stomach-churning roller coaster, trying to get any sleep felt impossible. Normally Dr. Jordan Flynn could sleep anywhere, anytime, as long as she wore her eye mask, had earplugs stuffed into her ears and soothing sounds were coming from the white-noise machine by her side. This time, though, none of it helped one bit.

Maybe it was because the top bunk of her cabin seemed to threaten to toss her out of it with every swell of the ship as it crossed the infamous Drake Passage on their way to Antarctica. Or because the noise machine's nature sounds were completely drowned out by real ones—the shrieking wind that she suspected no earplugs were heavy-duty enough to truly muffle.

She rolled to her side and it seemed the ship rolled along with her. Some people might pay big money to go on a crazy ride like this one at an amusement park, but at that moment, she'd pay even bigger money to get off it, if she could.

She squeezed her eyes closed behind the mask, then laughed at herself a little. Early October might be closer to bringing all-day sunlight to Antarctica, but she knew the low glow coming from a small window above her head wasn't what was keeping her awake. Trying to somehow force her mind away from the uncomfortable rolling sensations, she tried to think about the plus side of the adventure she was embarking on. And working as a doctor at an Antarctic science station would definitely be an adventure.

Fletcher Station was brand-new, and despite her current discomfort, she was still thankful she'd been chosen to work there as a surgeon and general practitioner for six months. Not only work there, but be the very first person to set up the medical clinic and hospital and get it ready for the thousand or so crew members who'd be arriving in a week or so. Plus, they'd seemed to love the idea of having the marine biologists test her parents' diving invention while they were underwater gathering samples, which was equally exciting.

Right now, only about seventy-five people were crossing the Drake Passage on this ship, getting things set up just like she was. Chefs and others prepping the kitchen and food, engineers getting machinery and equipment ready, and other support staff of all kinds. And, of course, a few scientists, with more on the way. Because scientific explorations, studies and discovery were the whole reason Fletcher Station existed.

Jordan thought about her little flat in London, her steady surgery job and her predictable life, which was exactly what she'd wanted when she'd decided to set down roots for the first time ever. Living all over the world with her doctor parents had been a great way to grow up, but she wanted something different for her adult life, and was happy with her choices.

She'd had to think hard about taking on this six-month stint in Antarctica. Then had decided, why not? One of these days, she expected that her roots would deepen and grow to include a husband and family, living in the same house together forever and ever. Until then, though, she'd enjoy this adventure, take care of patients and get further testing of her parents' diving invention, one that would hopefully solve the problem of barotrauma. Doing a trial on how well it worked in Antarctica's extremely cold water as compared to other places would be another strong step toward getting it on the market.

The boat tossed hard, and to focus on something besides the rough ride, she tried to visualize what the medical center would look like, and how much would be involved in getting the equipment set up. Then, inexplicably, that picture was interrupted by an absurdly handsome face floating in her mind's eye. A face that belonged to the man in the cabin next door.

She'd been trying to get her door unlocked, hanging on to the doorjamb with one hand so she could stay upright, when he'd rounded a corner and strode down the hallway toward the door next to hers. He'd paused, with the key in his hand, to send her a charming smile and ask if she needed help.

She'd given him a quick smile back and a "No, thanks" before she finally got the door unlocked and opened. She'd stepped inside and bolted it, relieved to climb up on the bunk and not have to wonder if she'd fall down before she got there.

Making small talk with anyone while working to keep her balance and swallow down a slight queasiness hadn't seemed very appealing. But now, in the rolling darkness of her cabin, his tall, muscular body, dark skin and deep brown eyes seemed to float in front of her. Eyes that held humor and intelligence, and a hint of a twinkle that had drawn her in the second she'd looked at him. Had even sent her heart into a ridiculous and unwelcome flutter.

She frowned, wondering why in the world she was thinking about a guy she didn't know. The deepening pitch of the boat had her grabbing the metal rungs at the top of the bed and holding on. Good thing she wasn't prone to full-on seasickness, or she'd probably be crawling her way to the bathroom by now.

Maybe sleeping on the top bunk hadn't been the best idea. With the way the boat swayed, she'd been afraid that the equipment she'd brought would slide across the floor, or be dislodged from the top bed, so she'd secured it on the lower bunk. Probably, though, being higher made her feel the pitch of the boat more than she would otherwise. Just as she was pondering if maybe she should just try to sleep somewhere on the floor, the storm sent the boat into its deepest roll yet. First one direction, then the other, then back so suddenly and violently she was flung from the bunk.

Her brain took a second to compute that she was airborne at the same time an automatic shriek left her lips. When her body reached the other side of the tiny cabin, her head connected with the wall as she slammed into it before dropping hard onto the floor like a rag doll thrown by a toddler. "Ow! Damn it!"

Dazed, she lay there a moment. The bruises on her elbow and shoulder started to complain. Her head throbbed. Something warm slid onto her forehead, and she lifted a shaking hand, coming into contact with sticky blood. She shoved off her eye mask and felt around her hairline, confirming that her darned head was cut open. Carefully moving her fingers to figure out where exactly the blood was coming from, and to gauge how much was oozing, she determined it was a fairly small trickle. Must not be too bad a gash since scalps normally bled a lot, so nothing to stress over too much.

She drew a shaky breath before gingerly sitting up. Figuring out what first aid might be necessary and how to actually accomplish it wasn't going to be easy. Did she even have a mirror in here to try to look at it?

Three loud raps on her door had her turning to stare at the gray metal panel and blink. It also made her realize that one of her earplugs had fallen out, even though she was sure she'd have heard that banging through double sets of the foam things.

Breathing deeply through her nose again, she tried to compose herself and removed the other plug, too, shakily shoving it into her pocket.

"Hey! You okay? Let me in."

Great. She closed her eyes and slumped back against the cabin wall. She'd bet good money that was her sexy neighbor's voice. Last thing she wanted was to have him touching her head and making her feel all fluttery, which she had a bad feeling might happen again, considering she'd been thinking of him just moments ago. But of course that was ridiculous. Attractive? Yes. But so were a lot of other men on this ship. And all were men who traveled for their work, and that she didn't have interest in.

Jordan opened her mouth to say she was fine, but as the blood trickled on down to her eyebrow, she had to grudgingly face reality. It made a whole lot more sense to let him see what was going on with her head wound than her trying to figure out how to check it herself. In a dark cabin with no mirrors, while the seas threw the boat around like a toy.

"Okay." She tried to stand, but realized she felt surprisingly shaky, which wasn't helped by the pitching of the boat. She ended up crawling to the door, feeling a little foolish as she reached up to unlock the knob, then leaned back against the wall next to it. "Come in."

The door crept open only a few inches, which she realized was smart on his part. Easy to accidentally bash someone if you shoved it wide open without first figuring out where they were. She could see him scan the room, then quickly look down, his brows rising and his eyes deep with concern even in the low light of the room.

"Are you hurt?" He flipped on the light switch, then crouched down next to her, his hand on the doorjamb to keep himself steady as the boat rolled. "I heard a loud thud, then somebody—you—cry out. What happened?"

"Got thrown from my bunk. Banged up. My head is bleeding, but just a little. Will you take a look and see what's going on up there?"

Another violent roll had her sliding sideways several inches on her rear, and his arm shot out to grab hers. "Let's get you off this floor and onto the lower bunk, since it's the only thing screwed down to the floor."

"No room. I have a bunch of equipment and stuff secured on there."

"Now there's a good idea. Keep the equipment safer on the lower bunk than your body and head." A disgusted sound left his mouth. "Hang tight. I'll be right back."

She leaned her aching head back against

the wall, hoping this wasn't a bad omen to start the trip. Then again, some of the craziest and worst stuff that had happened to her and her parents on their working treks around the world later made for some of the best stories and laughs.

At the sound of his feet coming up the hall, she turned to see him staggering into the cabin with an armload of bedding while the boat tipped deeply to one side again, and she couldn't seem to keep from sliding back the other direction. "I'm going to tuck you into this corner over here so you'll be still while I take a look."

"Little Jordan Horner sat in a corner eating her curds and whey," she muttered.

"You're getting your nursery rhymes mixed up. Not to mention that's a little weird." He picked her up in his arms like she weighed nothing and gently sat her in the corner, stuffing the bedding on both sides of her hips, instantly making her feel more secure. "You feel nauseated? Confused?"

"I'm pretty sure I don't have a concussion," she said, wincing as she lifted her fingers to touch the tender lump on her head. "And feeling nauseated would be a given, considering the way the ship's been rolling for the past who knows how many hours."

"True." He shot her that smile that made her feel a little weak in the knees. "I'm Ezekiel Edwards, by the way. Friends call me Zeke."

"Jordan Flynn."

"I know. Fletcher Station's doctor." He nodded. "I'm a marine biologist and climatologist. PhD. Also a trained medic, so you can trust me to take care of your head."

"How do you know I'm the station's doctor?"

"Saw your name on the roster. And okay, true confessions." That quick smile again. "Someone on this ship told me the doctor on board was drop-dead gorgeous, and as soon as I saw you in the hall earlier, I knew it had to be you."

"Is this your usual chitchat when you meet a woman?" She rolled her eyes, not even close to surprised about that, then regretted it when it made her head hurt worse.

He chuckled. "It's just nice to finally meet you." He pulled a flashlight from his pocket and kneeled in front of her, lifting her chin to look in her eyes.

"Honestly, I don't have a concussion."

"How do you know? Do you usually recite nursery rhymes just for the hell of it?"

"Actually, yes. It was something my parents taught me to do when I felt worried about something, or if I was hurt, to distract me." And right now, she seemed to need a distraction from his chiseled features and sexy lips and the manly way he smelled, way more than from her bruised body and the movement of the boat.

"Huh. That's a new one." He gave her a crooked smile as his thumb moved from her chin and slipped across her cheek before dropping away. "Lean your head down so I can see what's going on with your injury."

His mouth was so close to her face she could feel his warm breath on her skin as his fingers gently moved through her hair. Her heart beat a little faster, and she had a bad feeling it was from his nearness and not her injuries. If she lifted her head back up, her lips would be in the perfect position to come into contact with his and…and…

Not happening, she reminded herself, scowling at how stupid she was being. She didn't even know the man. Why was she feeling this serious attraction in the middle of a storm while she had a busted-open head? Maybe she had a concussion, after all. Or brain damage.

"It's not too bad," Zeke said as his fingers touched around the rest of her scalp, obviously looking for more lumps or cuts, his voice a deep rumble against her face. "I have some derma glue, which will fix it right up."

"I have some, too. In that blue box on the bed."

"Good. I need to get this washed first. Sit tight while I get some stuff."

Sitting in the corner with the boat moving side to side made her stomach decide to complain even more. Probably it had something to do with her bruises and bleeding, too, but either way, it was bad. Bad that she felt sick, and bad that it was looking like she just might vomit right in front of the world's sexiest man.

Her eyes popped open in horror at the thought. Wildly, she looked around to see if there was something, anything, within reach she could barf into before he got back. Relief filled her chest when she saw a metal trash can sliding a few inches across the floor as the boat rolled again, and she stretched over as far as she could, desperately wiggling her fingers to try to grab the rim. Before she could get her hand on it, Zeke came back into the room and she stared up at him, a full-blown panic starting to fill her chest over the situation.

"Um… Can you…go away…and…come back in a little bit?"

That smile she'd already fallen for slowly stretched his mouth until his teeth shone white against his dark skin. "Feeling seasick? In a storm like this, that's totally normal. Not to mention you're hurt, which also can make you queasy, as I'm sure you know. Here."

He set the stuff he was carrying on the floor and put the trash can in her hands. She glared at him as her stomach roiled. Swallowing hard, she knew she couldn't control it much longer. "Can't you see I need some privacy? Go away, please!"

"Don't worry. I've seen plenty of sick people on this exact boat. No point in fighting it. You'll feel better, then I'll get your head fixed up."

"I don't—" Oh, Lord, she couldn't hold it

back any longer, totally mortified as she got sick into the can.

He stroked her hair, rubbed her back, talking the whole time in a soothing voice. She wasn't sure what he said, and also wasn't sure if his sweetness endeared him to her even more or made her want to hit him for not leaving her alone like she'd asked. What a way to get to know a guy.

Except she didn't want to get to know him, right? Trying to think of this horror as a potentially positive thing, she gave up trying to hold it back and got sick all over again.

Finally, the awful feeling subsided. She went to wipe her mouth, avoiding looking at him, and he tucked a damp cloth into her hand along with a tin of mints. He disappeared with the trash can and she was torn between feeling beyond embarrassed he was having to play nurse, and grateful that he was getting rid of the mess. In minutes, he was back and reaching into the box he'd brought.

"You feeling up to me cleaning your head? I can wait if you're not ready."

"Ready." Or as ready as she was going

to be, with his body so close and his hands touching her, her embarrassment warring with a quivery feeling that had nothing to do with being tossed around the boat or with feeling sick and being injured.

With a last swipe of the cloth across her mouth, she popped one of the mints. Feeling marginally better, and glad to have minty fresh breath instead of the prior awful taste in her mouth, she leaned her head against the wall to let him take care of the first aid she needed. Whatever he'd put on the gauze stung as he cleaned the wound. He obviously knew what he was doing, working slowly and gently, but she still couldn't help but wince.

"Hang in there. I know it hurts. Almost done with this part. Then I'll glue it."

"Why do you have derma glue?"

"Did you think I was lying when I said I'm a trained medic?"

"I…forgot. Did you become a medic first, then decide to get your PhDs in marine biology and whatever else you said? Or the other way around?" she asked, as much to distract herself as because she wanted to know.

"I grew up in a place where knowing first

aid came in handy." That seemed like an odd answer, and just as she was going to ask him what he meant, he continued. "Now I spend a lot of time in potentially dangerous waters and up mountain ranges and glaciers, like here in Antarctica. Cuts on coral, and bites and stings from sea life, or falls and other injuries, happen sometimes despite good planning. You better know what to do to treat yourself, or the people with you."

She nodded, and he cursed in response. "Hold still. I'm about to put the glue on now to close it. The cut's barely an inch long, so won't take but a second. Don't. Move."

She steeled herself, but didn't need to because she didn't feel a thing. "Thanks so much for everything. I…really appreciate it. Trying to clean it and glue it myself wouldn't have been easy."

"Hopefully, I won't need your assistance the same way, Dr. Flynn, but we never know, do we?" He gave her another knee-weakening smile before he stood, his legs wide to keep his balance. "Stay put for a minute. I'm going to move everything off the lower bunk and secure it somewhere else, so you can sleep there instead of the top bunk."

She opened her mouth to protest, because some of the equipment was delicate. If any of it got broken, it would take a long time for more to be sent on a future ship. Then she realized that he was right, and she trusted him to make sure everything would be kept safe. Must be the calm strength and confidence that simply oozed from the man.

She knew she'd sleep better, assuming she slept at all, if she was only a foot from the floor. And the last thing her banged-up body needed was another jolt out of that top bed. If that happened, she might not be able to get the clinic and hospital ready to go before the next ships arrived.

"Thank you. Again."

"You'll find we're all a team here. No need to thank me for anything."

In no time, he had everything off the bed and secured as well as possible, the covers pulled aside, then came back to her. She felt strangely comfortable tucked into her corner with all that bedding and wasn't sure she wanted to go back to that bunk. Except it was probably Zeke's own bedding wrapped around her. He doubtless needed it back, or neither one of them would get any sleep.

"Okay. Bed's ready."

His arms moved to slide beneath her legs and back, and her independent side kicked in, knowing she shouldn't let him carry her again.

"I'm… I can walk."

"I'm sure you can. But why would you, when you're probably shaky and the boat is still moving all over the place and I'm here?"

"Well… I admit my head is throbbing, and I don't much feel like staggering across the room right now."

"Appreciate a sensible woman."

He lifted her against his wide chest and held her close as he stepped to the bunk to lay her on it, then pulled the covers up to her chin. She had to smile even as she felt a little ridiculous. "You're making me feel like a little kid with a boo-boo."

"Want me to tell you a nursery rhyme?" He smiled down at her, and her heart beat a little harder as their gazes met and held.

Somehow, she shook herself out of the trance that Zeke Edwards seemed to put her in all too easily. "Not necessary, thanks. But can you do me one more favor?"

"What's that?"

"My eye mask is somewhere on the floor near the door."

"Eye mask?" He barked out a laugh. "Is it filled with cucumber essence to keep you bright and beautiful?"

"Funny. It's great for travel, so don't knock it until you've tried it. Makes me feel like I'm in a little cocoon, along with the foam earplugs I wear. Helps me sleep on long journeys or in strange places."

"Can I borrow yours to try?"

That grin and the humor in his eyes tugged her mouth into a reluctant return smile. "Yes, because I always have at least two with me on a trip. Just in case."

Another chuckle as he picked the eye mask up from the floor and brought it to her, carefully sliding it over the top of her head before adjusting it to cover her eyes.

"Sleep tight, Jordan Flynn."

"Good night, Zeke." Jordan lay there still and quiet until she heard the click of the door.

Well, damn.

Yeah, she just might be in trouble here, but no way was she falling for a guy like Ezekiel Edwards. She wasn't a fling kind of woman, and her next relationship would be with a steady man who wanted to share a perfect little house with a picket fence in a lovely neighborhood. Live in the same place for years and years, and have a few children who'd get to see their cousins and grandparents all the time. Grow up with the same friends their whole lives.

Antarctica was not the place she'd find her future husband who wanted the same things she did, only men like Zeke who traveled the world for their work just as her parents had.

She fished her single earplug from her pocket, having no idea where the other one had ended up, and stuffed it in her ear. Tried to eliminate thoughts of Zeke from her mind, without success. But it would be okay. Once at Fletcher Station they'd both be busy and she'd have no trouble steering clear of him, except in the most superficial, coworker way.

She was sure of it. And never mind that her body still tingled from his touch.

CHAPTER TWO

THE ROLLING OF the boat lasted all night and into the next morning, and when the storm finally subsided, Zeke drew a deep breath of relief. He had trouble sleeping no matter where he was, and figured that, between the deep, rocking waves and her poor, sore head, Jordan probably hadn't gotten much, either.

When Captain John Stewart announced over the loudspeaker that everyone was now allowed out of their cabins for lunch before they docked, Zeke couldn't wait to get some fresh air. Out in the hallway he paused, wondering if it would be too pushy to knock on Jordan's door to see how she was doing. He decided that, since she'd had a head injury, it was perfectly acceptable for him to check on her.

He rapped on the door. "Jordan? Zeke. Wondering how you're feeling."

"I'm fine." Her voice was muffled, but she sounded fine. Very fine, just like the rest of her. "Thanks again for your help last night."

"You're welcome." He stuck his hands in his pockets, wondering if she'd invite him in. Waited for the door to open so he could see her pretty face and deep blue eyes. When it didn't, he was surprised and annoyed at how disappointed he felt. Probably shouldn't be, though, since thinking of her just one cabin over, and how she'd felt in his arms, had been part of the reason he'd been awake half the night. "So, I guess I'll see you around."

"'Kay."

With that clear dismissal, he shook off the odd feeling and headed to the deck to breathe in the now-calmer wind and talk with people he knew. The main conversation was about last night and how it had been one of the worst Drake Passage storms they'd been through, which morphed into everyone trying to one-up each other with nightmare sea stories from their pasts.

Grinning at the good-natured arguments

and obvious exaggerations, he decided to head to the bridge to find out how much longer they'd be until landfall.

"What's with the roll of this tub?" he asked John as he stepped through the door. "Two days ago, you said it looked like smooth sailing. Pretty sure last night didn't qualify."

John laughed, but kept his eyes on the gently rolling swells in front of them. "Sorry. It was one of those times when the weather changed in the blink of an eye. But we're at a steady twenty knots now, and I think it'll stay there until we get to shore."

"Says the man convinced it would be Lake Drake this whole trip, flat as a pancake." He thought about Jordan getting hurt flying out of her bunk and pondered telling John about it, since, as captain, he'd want to know. But he had a feeling Jordan wouldn't want a bunch of questions about it, and he'd look at her head when he had a chance. No need to have John check on her when Zeke could do it himself.

"Yeah, well, it takes a big man to admit that sometimes he's wrong," John said, "and I pride myself on being pretty big."

Zeke chuckled, knowing he was referring to his girth as much as anything. "How long until we get there?"

"About…" He peered at the dials, then the horizon. "Forty-five minutes."

"That soon? You told everyone they could come to the lounge for lunch, but there won't be time for that."

"We made better time than I expected. The plus side of the winds and currents we had last night. But we've got lunch all ready, so we're still going to hand it out to those who want it." John shrugged. "Just sandwiches, though. It was all the kitchen crew could put together with the weather we had, and I didn't know when it would clear up. So I told them to go ahead and make a sandwich lunch. Trying to eat bacon and eggs from a plate isn't easy when the ship's all over the place, as you know."

"Sandwich sounds good. Thanks. I'll grab one before I get all my equipment pulled together. Appreciate the ride, such as it was."

"Anytime." John grinned as they shook hands. "See you the other way in…what? Six months?"

"That's the plan, unless I have to leave

earlier to make sure my next grant gets approved. See you then."

Zeke headed to the lounge to make sure he got one of the sandwiches, since he suddenly realized he was hungry, not having had much for dinner. An empty stomach in stormy seas wasn't a good thing, but neither was a full one, and he'd tried to find the right balance before he'd headed to bed.

Thinking of how he'd startled awake with a pounding heart when he'd heard Jordan slam against that wall, then cry out, had him wanting to check on her again. Except she'd made it clear she didn't want that, so he planned to do the next best thing, which was to be a considerate guy and grab a sandwich for her, too. After getting sick last night, and everything else, she was probably starving.

The moment he walked into the lounge, his gaze went straight to the tall, slender woman with shiny dark hair to her shoulders. She was standing next to the rows of wrapped sandwiches, and his heart did a strange little pit-a-pat to see her there.

Apparently, he'd been right. Jordan was indeed hungry.

He moved to stand next to her, leaning

down. "I'm a fan of the Reubens, but the turkey with bacon is good, too."

"I thought about getting the veggie, but saw it has raw onions. Yuck."

The way she cutely screwed up her face in obvious distaste made him smile. "I'm with you. Raw onions on a sandwich is a solid *no* for me."

"Yes. A solid *no*." Her mouth relaxed into a wide grin, and he realized it was the first full smile he'd seen from her. He liked the way it made her deep blue eyes twinkle, and a dimple poke into one cheek. "Any idea when we'll be docking?"

"Captain Stewart said about forty-five minutes. Less than that now. So before we do, I want to take a look at your head. How's it feel?"

"Honestly? It hurts. Way more than last night. But that's to be expected of a gash and bruise like that."

"Let's go out on the deck so I can see it."

"It's fine."

"You just said it hurts."

"Like there's something you can do about that? Just needs time to heal, that's all."

"So, when you have a patient that refuses

to let you follow up after their treatment, you nod and are perfectly okay with that? I just want to look at the glue job, and see if it seems to be holding well." He wasn't sure why he felt so frustrated at her stubbornness. She was a surgeon, after all, and knew all about wounds and derma glue, and if she wanted to deal with it herself, what was it to him?

Maybe because the sound of her hitting that wall in the middle of the night had woken him from the terrifying dreams he sometimes endured, and he still felt a little unsettled by all of it. Wasn't it normal to want to check on her now, to make sure she was really okay?

For long seconds, her gaze clashed with his, until she released an exaggerated sigh. "Okay, fine. But can we please find a place where not everyone on the ship is going to be coming up to us and asking what happened?"

So he'd been right that she wouldn't want John, or anyone else, making too big a deal of her injury, and what happened last night.

"I know a good spot."

He nearly reached for her hand, but was

pretty sure she wouldn't appreciate the familiarity, even though they'd shared an unusual closeness last night. He stuck his fist into his coat pocket instead. Most people were at the bow of the ship to see Antarctica in the distance, so Zeke led the way to the back of the boat and around a corner where they'd be alone.

Wind whipped her soft hair into her face and she reached back to gather it into a ponytail behind her head. He tried not to get distracted by the beautiful line of her jaw that he'd noticed in the low light of her cabin last night.

He drew in a breath and put his hands on either side of her head, tipping it slightly down. Moved her hair gently out of the way so he could see the wound. A raw, red line spanned the bruised lump that resembled a miniature purple eggplant just above her hairline. But the edges of the gash seemed firmly closed together, and it obviously hadn't bled during the night, so it seemed the glue had done its job.

"Looks like it hurts like hell. But the good news is the wound is still nicely closed, so unless you whack it again, it should heal just fine."

"I thought it felt secured, but couldn't be sure." She gave him a twisted smile that showed she knew her stubbornness a moment ago about her dealing with herself hadn't made a lot of sense. "Thanks again for patching me up."

Shocked by an urge to press a soft kiss to her head, he dropped his hands and stepped back. "I'm going to check with the captain, see when it would be okay to go below and start to gather my gear, which is going to take a while. If I see you, I'll give you the heads-up on how close we are so you can pull yours together, too."

"Thanks. Appreciate that."

An awkward silence fell between them, and he gave her what he hoped was a relaxed smile before moving to the bridge to get the information he needed from John. He wished he had eyes in the back of his head to see if she was watching him go. Because he sure as hell knew if she'd been the one walking off, his attention would have been riveted until she was out of sight.

Jordan Flynn was a beauty, no doubt

about it. But he hadn't had any kind of real relationship since he'd broken it off with his last girlfriend after the worst week of his life, and didn't plan to go there ever again.

John gave him the go-ahead, and he went below to the cargo area to search for the boxes of dive equipment and everything else he needed. Being one of the first to get his gear on the shuttle meant it wouldn't have to follow him during the next round of supplies-toting when the shuttle got full, and he began stacking everything onto several carts.

A cardboard sign caught his eye as he moved his first cart to the huge exit doors so he'd be at the front of the pack. Large letters printed in orange noted the multiple boxes that held medical equipment for the clinic and hospital.

He hesitated. Should he help Jordan out by stacking it on some of the empty carts and getting it ready so her stuff would be on the first shuttles out, too? Being a newbie on these expeditions, she wouldn't know that it could be another full day before the medical gear got delivered to the station if it didn't go out on the first round.

He shook his head at himself. Being helpful when someone needed it was all well and good, but at what point did it border on being a busybody, or even a creep? No, his own stuff was plenty to deal with right now. The crew was there to help Jordan. If he ran into her while they were both still on the ship, he'd give her the heads-up about how things worked around here. Otherwise, he'd mind his own business, and concentrate on work, like he always did.

With the ship nearing shore, Jordan hurried to the bow with dozens of others wanting to admire the scenery before they disembarked, so excited to get her first glimpses of the place she'd be calling home for the next six months. She'd seen so many photographs of the shoreline, and the icebergs and sea creatures that could be sighted, and each one had seemed more incredible than the last. She nearly had to pinch herself that she was about to experience it for real.

Standing on the open deck with the cold wind on her face thankfully much less ferocious than the day before, Jordan grasped the handrail and wondered if Zeke Edwards was somewhere within the crowd, too. Though why she couldn't get her mind off the man, she had no idea. Whether she wanted to or not, though, she'd be lying to herself if she didn't admit she wished he was standing there next to her, talking to her in that beautiful bass voice and charming American accent of his about this amazing world she was about to enter.

She stared out at one of the incredible white mountains of ice in the water, one side gleaming with a blue so deeply iridescent it took her breath away. It seemed fairly close to the ship, but she suspected that was an illusion, that it was actually much farther away than it appeared. Other flat icebergs floated nearby with groups of seals lounging on them. She knew Antarctica was home to dozens of species, but had no idea what kind these were. Wouldn't it be helpful if a certain marine biologist with warm eyes and an all-too-appealing smile was there to educate her about some of the wildlife she was seeing?

"Pretty, isn't it?"

Her heart jolted, then sped up. As though she'd conjured him with her thoughts, Zeke

Edwards stood next to her, his face tipped down toward hers, his mouth relaxed into a small smile. The cold air stung her lungs as she breathed in and smiled back, and suddenly the incredible images in front of her seemed even more staggeringly beautiful.

"Pretty? It's incredible."

"The icebergs are truly wonders. Some are so big, hundreds and even thousands of feet thick and miles wide, that they're given names and tracked. Captain Stewart is giving this one a wide berth because sonar doesn't show if there might be a lot of ice reaching horizontally under the water. Don't want to end up like the *Titanic*."

"An even bigger accident than my small one last night is not the way I want to go. Thrown into freezing water, fingers and toes quickly numbing from hypothermia. Then convulsions, mental disorientation, organ failure. Finally, death. I hope to get to see more of Antarctica before that would happen."

A laugh rumbled from his chest as his amused eyes met hers. "Showing off your medical knowledge, Dr. Flynn?"

"Always do, whenever the opportunity arises."

The way they were smiling at one another, taking her back to that intimate feeling last night, sent her heart into a silly pit-a-pat.

"Glad to hear that. Upping my education on all things medical is something I enjoy." A strand of her hair insisted on flying into her eyes, and his finger reached to tuck it back inside her hat. "Good news is I think you're safe from hypothermia at the moment. Ship has neoprene immersion suits on board, and lifeboats. We're close enough to shore that we'd make it before the death phase."

"Thank heavens I can stop worrying now." Again, that chuckle rumbled from his chest, warming hers. "I've lived in a lot of places around the world, but usually in hot locations. Freezing to death is something I hope to avoid."

"Why have you lived lots of places around the world?"

"My parents are both doctors who work for an international organization that took us all over. It was an interesting way to grow up, but I'm glad to be done with it. Never had the comfort of living in one place, having the same friends for years and being close to grandparents and extended family. So I'm happy to finally be putting down roots somewhere."

Oddly, he didn't respond after getting her answer, his expression strangely serious.

"So." The awkward silence had her wanting to fill it with more chitchat. "Do you travel a lot for your work?"

"Yes. Various places, but for a marine biologist and climatologist, Antarctica holds the most interesting discoveries. I've been here thirteen times."

"Thirteen times?" Wow, the man was nearly as rootless as her parents. "You come more than once a year?"

"Sometimes. What we're learning here about the climate changes in the world is invaluable."

"I'm embarrassed to admit I don't know exactly what a marine biologist does. Other than study the ocean."

"We study the ocean floor and gather samples. Collect data on how warming and acidification of the polar waters is affecting all kinds of life, from the smallest plankton to penguins."

"And climatology?"

"Interconnected, but that involves gathering ice cores aboveground, among other things. I usually focus on either land or sea on each trip. The goal is to gather enough data to make private companies and governments see that significant changes need to happen to slow down the warming of our planet."

The passion in his eyes was intense, and she wondered how he'd decided to do that kind of research. She opened her mouth to ask more questions when a young man came to stand behind her, and she turned to look at him.

"Excuse me, are you Dr. Flynn?"

"Yes."

"Captain Stewart told me to load your equipment onto transport carts. Help you get it off the ship and onto the shuttle. It's ready to go down in the cargo hold as soon as we land."

She'd hoped there might be a few crew members in the cargo space that would be able to help her pull all the bulky equipment together, but hadn't counted on it. To hear it was already loaded up was a big, but pleasant, surprise.

"Well, thank you. Should I meet you down there?"

"Yes, ma'am. I'll be at cargo door three."

The young man left and she turned back to Zeke. "Wow, that's a nice surprise. I wasn't sure how much help I'd have, and there's a lot of stuff to take. The amount of equipment and supplies they gave me to open up the medical center is crazy. I'll have to thank Captain Stewart for thinking about it."

"He'd appreciate that."

Something about the expression in his eyes and the way he rocked back on his heels with his hands in his pockets struck her as slightly odd, and suddenly she knew why.

"It was you, wasn't it? You're the one who asked him to help me!"

"No. I asked Captain Stewart to see who might be able to give you a hand."

"I don't want to be treated differently from other people just because I'm a woman. It's my job to—"

"Jordan. There are times to be independent, and times to let people help. And it has nothing to do with you being a woman." His dark eyes met hers. "I already told you how many times I've been down here. If you don't get your stuff off the boat on the first round, you'll be waiting for it for another day or two. And since you wouldn't know that, and you'll be wanting to get the clinic and hospital set up as soon as possible, I figured I'd grease the wheels a bit so you'll be ready in case of a medical emergency."

A confusing mix of frustration and gratitude filled her chest. She did need to get everything set up as soon as possible, both because she had to begin doing baseline physicals on everyone who'd arrived in this first round, and also in case there was an emergency, as he'd said. But it sure seemed like the man was a little controlling.

She drew a deep breath. "I appreciate that, and admit I'll be glad to have everything at the station. But I would have liked for you to have given me the heads-up so I could be the one asking the crew for help. As the station's doctor, people need to know I'm fully capable of dealing with whatever I have to deal with here."

"My apologies for not talking to you first." He reached out to shake her hand, and even through her glove she could swear she felt the warmth of his hand clear down to her toes. "Good luck with your clinic setup—that's going to be a big job. Don't let that independent streak of yours keep you from asking me or someone else for help, okay? See you around."

She held her now-empty hand in her other one and watched his long legs jog down the metal stairs of the boat, probably going below to the cargo area to get his own things ready.

What was it about the man that had her feeling all wound up? Slightly irritated and ridiculously attracted?

She blew out a breath. There was zero point in being attracted to him. He lived the kind of life she'd left behind. This trip was about caring for patients and testing her parents' device, right? When the time came that she wanted to become interested in a man, it was going to happen back home in London. Period.

CHAPTER THREE

Satisfied that all the scuba gear and other diving equipment had been scrutinized, confirmed to be in good working order and organized, Zeke moved on to get the new aquarium room built and everything installed that he and the other marine biologists would need for their samples. He'd never had to do this in Antarctica before. Usually, all the science stations had everything set up already, needing only some adjusting and tweaking.

But Fletcher Station was brand-new, and while starting from scratch would be a lot of work, it gave him a chance to create something better than what someone else had built. He got to work, and hours passed as he carefully set the rock work in place, then got the salt water prepared. Assembled the various hoses, filters and everything else the aquarium needed to support the marine life he'd be bringing here to study. He paused to stretch, pleased to be making good progress on this big job.

"Glad to see you're halfway done here, so you can't drag me into doing your work, and mine, too."

Zeke looked toward the door. Bob Shamansky, who worked for the same Southern California university he did, stood there holding a cardboard box in his arms.

"I'm pretty sure it's usually the other way around," Zeke said. "You asking me to bring up who knows what from the seafloor for you to study instead of learning how to dive so you can do it yourself?"

"Why should I learn to dive when I have people like you to do it for me?" Bob grinned as he set the box on one of the long tables lining the outer wall. "Besides, you don't fool me. Diving is your favorite part of the job."

"One of my favorites, I admit. You don't know what you're missing."

"I'll stay in the lab and you macho types

can go dive into dark ice-cold water—
thanks, anyway."

"Hey, I read about your latest break-
through with a medicine you created through
halogens in seawater. Treats neurological
disorders, doesn't it? Congratulations."

"Thanks. Happy about it. Took me about
five years from creation through the clinical
trials to finally get it approved. Your samples helped make it happen, so congrats to
you, too."

Another reminder of why the work they
all did here was so important, and Zeke's
fatigue slipped away as he turned back to
the aquarium tasks. "What's on your list of
things for me to collect this time?"

"I'll tell you about it after we get set up.
This study is something totally new, and I'm
pretty pumped about it."

"Which I know means you're giving me
some tough jobs." Zeke grinned. "You need
help carrying anything in?"

"I've got a crew guy giving me a hand
down in the storage hangar, then he's going
to help bring it here after the Ski-Doo training. Which I think I saw is in about an hour.
Want to race?"

"We'd get in trouble with the station head for being a bad influence on the newbies."

"Well, dang it. Since we'll be at twenty-four hours of daylight in no time we won't be able to race in the dark, so he can't see us. Risking falling in a crevasse is such a thrill."

"Says the man who won't even go diving. You're all talk, Shamansky."

"True. I'm about as risk averse as they come." He clapped Zeke on the back. "Going to grab my cart and bring it up. See you at the training."

"You'll be easy to spot, if you still wear that blue top hat over a balaclava."

"I traded it in for an orange one this year. And something else, but you'll have to come to the practice to find out what it is."

Zeke shook his head and chuckled as Bob left the room, turning back to his work. Digging in the plastic containers he'd brought up here, he realized he didn't have some of the tubing and filters he needed. A lot of his gear was still in the storage hangar, but several of the boxes were crammed beneath his bed.

He glanced at his watch. Since his cabin was about halfway between here and where they'd be conducting the Ski-Doo practice, he might as well see if what he needed was there to save time on his way back. He made his way through a covered, aboveground bridge that connected this building to Pod B where he'd be bunking. He moved down a hallway past rows of doors until he found his small cabin. With one single bed, a small table he used as a desk and built-in closet for clothes, it was comfortable enough. Good thing, since he'd be calling this place home for the next six months.

Home. He tried not to think about the home where he'd grown up. That it didn't exist anymore, and neither did his parents. Or the other two people he'd loved and who'd raised him after his parents died. Home was San Diego now, or at least as much of a home as he ever wanted to have again.

But there was no point in going over all that again. He'd learned what he'd had to about himself from that horrible experience, and would never forget.

He rolled up the shade covering the small window so he could look out over the ice fields beyond. In the summer months of endless sun, the light-blocking shades were essential to a good night's sleep, which he had trouble achieving even when it was dark. The shades took his mind back to Jordan Flynn and her eye mask, and he had to smile, thinking about her spunk and her shiny hair and deep blue eyes the color of the Pacific.

He turned and grabbed the things he needed from one of the boxes, put on the standard-issue red snowsuit the station had given everyone, then headed for the Ski-Doo practice. Pointless that it was, he couldn't seem to help the sudden spring in his step, knowing he'd see Jordan there.

Jordan stood near the big snow machines, deciding they looked a lot like motorcycles, and if that was the case, she'd be okay riding one. Living in so many unusual situations and places, she was probably more experienced driving all kinds of vehicles than most people, and hopefully this wouldn't be anything particularly new or different.

With her peripheral vision, she noted a tall form approaching. Despite wearing the same red snowsuit as everyone else out there, she knew without even looking that it was Ezekiel Edwards, and frowned at the way her heart beat a little faster. Couldn't help feeling that, when his gaze met hers, a small smile on his lips, it all somehow seemed to warm the freezing air.

"Ready for the Ski-Doo instruction?" he asked. "Have you ridden one before?"

"Not exactly. Motorcycles and scooters and such, yes. I told you my life experiences have been mostly in hot places, except for England. I'm guessing they're a lot like a Jet Ski?"

"Except without waves to hit and maneuver over. Here, you just have to make sure you don't drive over a crevasse and disappear deep inside, or get too close to the edge of an ice shelf and have it crack off so you end up in frigid water. Experiencing that hypothermia and death you talked about."

"You're making that up."

"Why do you think they have practice? There's a lot involved in knowing the safest ways to get around the area, especially if you're going out in the field."

"Well, that makes me glad they're doing this, to train newbies like me."

"I'd offer you help, but I know how you react to that. Don't want you annoyed with me again." His eyes crinkled at the corners as his smile widened. "Good luck and have fun."

She watched him move toward one of the Ski-Doos, and found herself still watching him as he slung one long leg over the saddle, got settled, then let it roar. She shook herself from the trance he seemed to send her into every darned time she was around him. When she was instructed to mount the machine and drive, she was more than glad to have something else to focus on besides how handsome and appealing the man was.

Relieved that she managed to get the machine started without any problems, she set out across the snow. Motor scooters and cycles were always fun, and riding the Ski-Doo was even better. Cold air tingling her face as she zoomed across the white world in front of her, maneuvering around the orange cones, had her deciding she'd definitely use this as transportation into the field whenever possible.

She brought hers to a stop to give someone else their turn to learn how to drive it, and her attention immediately slid to Zeke as he went through the obstacle course.

His obvious confidence as he operated the machine showed he was an expert driver, which wasn't a surprise since he said he'd been to Antarctica thirteen times. An incredible number since the man couldn't be more than thirty-five or so. He must have taken these trips sometimes twice in one year, unless he'd started doing this as an undergrad, and even then, it was impressive.

He pulled up next to her, sending that appealing smile her way. "Ready for the next lesson?"

"Yes. This is really fun."

"Next part is less fun, and a lot trickier, but essential to know when you're away from the base."

Zeke's gaze moved past her, and when he started laughing, she turned to see a man wearing an orange top hat that looked like something out of *Alice in Wonderland*, and a scarf with polar bears all over it wrapped around his neck.

"Good look for you, Bob!" Zeke called. "Though you know some of the newbies are going to expect to see polar bears here now."

The man responded with a laugh and a thumbs-up before Zeke turned back to Jordan with a grin. "Bob Shamansky. Works for the same university I do."

"That hat would be a good look on you, too," she said. In truth, she found that impossible to picture, since Zeke Edwards simply oozed masculine sex appeal and sophistication. "But everyone who comes down here to work has to know polar bears only live around the north pole."

"You'd be surprised." He dismounted the machine and picked up a nearby pair of skis, leaning them against the snow machine. "Bob's a chemical biologist who creates new medicines—you might be interested in talking to him about some of them, Dr. Flynn."

"Really? I know marine life here can be used to create them. That's so interesting."

"It is. Now for the tricky part of the lesson." He pulled some rope from one of the storage boxes on the side of the Ski-Doo and handed them to Chip Chambers, the station head who'd been instructing everyone, as the crew all crowded around.

"Okay, everyone," Chip said. "It's important to know that crevasses are everywhere out in the field. Those of us who've been here a lot learn to look for signs of them, but when they're covered with blowing snow it's a lot trickier."

"Then how do you know if they're there?" one man asked.

"You can't always know. Which is why we try to have those less experienced travel into the field with someone who's done it a lot of times, and why we have strategies for when things go wrong." Chip held up the two ropes and began to tie them to the machine. "We attach these to the back, like so, set the throttle to a low speed and hold on as it travels, skiing behind it. If the machine heads into a crevasse, you have to release the ropes and just let it go."

"I'm not sure I know what you mean," another crew member said.

"I'll demonstrate." Chip sat sideways on the snowmobile, put the skis on, then to Jordan's surprise, he actually got the machine moving with the ropes trailing behind in the snow. "There's a kill switch right here. If you fall while you're skiing behind it, hit the switch to stop the machine. Once it's moving, stand up and pick up the ropes, like so, then let the skis take you until you're trailing along behind it."

As Jordan and the others watched him stand and let the moving snow machine and attached ropes tug him along on the skis until he was slowly pulled forward, she had a feeling he made it look easy. One of the young men—a guy who'd told her he worked in the kitchen—volunteered to try it, and she was glad, because she didn't want to be the first one and possibly end up on her face.

"Okay," Chip said. "Skis on, throttle going, stand to pick up the ropes, then move to ski behind it. Ready?"

"Ready."

Doing exactly as he'd been shown, it looked like it was going to be an easy ride. Until he pushed the throttle a little too fast, which made him hurry and stumble trying to grab the ropes. Jordan gasped when he got tangled up and went down onto the hard ice, shrieking in obvious pain as he was dragged a short distance before he let go.

"Hell," Zeke said, sprinting after the machine as it kept on going. Jordan and the station head ran to see how the man might have hurt himself.

She knelt down beside the guy, who was clutching his upper arm and rolling back and forth on the snow. "Tell me what hurts," she said.

"My arm. Shoulder. Damn it, I think it's broken."

"Maybe not. We'll see. But we need to go inside. It's too cold out here to take off your snowsuit and everything. What's your name?"

"Pete. Pete Sanders."

"Think you can walk, Pete?"

"I… Yeah."

"Damn it. I'm sorry this happened," Chip said. "But Dr. Flynn will take good care of you, I know."

Two people who'd been participating in the snowmobile practice came over to assist as Jordan and Chip carefully helped the man to his feet. As they moved toward the station, Zeke jogged up next to them, barely out of breath.

"Looks like you're doing okay. Hang in there. I'll take over for you, Chip."

"Thanks. I'll check on you as soon as I'm done here, Pete."

Chip moved away and Zeke held Pete steady as his dark eyes moved to meet Jordan's. "What did he hurt?"

"About to find out. Arm or shoulder, based on what he said."

"Are we taking him to the clinic? Is it ready?"

"Is that a real question, Mr. Field Medic?" She smiled. "It's not fully pulled together yet but ready to see patients. But you don't need to come."

"Might as well see if I can help, since you're alone there until the next boat arrives."

"Appreciate it." And she did. Much as she could handle whatever was going on alone if she had to, if something was broken or dislocated, having someone there to assist would be a big help, especially without a nurse.

"That was a pretty exciting maneuver there, Pete. Wish I'd gotten it on video," Zeke said as he kept a steadying hand behind Pete's back.

The man managed a weak laugh. "Yeah. I'm never going to hear the end of this."

"Being famous for crashing during the snowmobile practice is better than nobody knowing who you are, right? A good way to introduce yourself to the women at the base, who'll all feel sorry for you and ask how you're feeling."

"One way to look at it, I guess. Thanks for that."

"You're welcome."

Zeke grinned at Pete, and Jordan had to smile at the way he was taking Pete's mind off his pain, which she had no doubt had been his goal.

As they moved through the long building, he proved to be a big help even before they got to the clinic, since he knew where to find an elevator so they could avoid most of the stairs. A good thing, because she'd been a little worried that the patient might be feeling light-headed and have trouble with that kind of exertion.

"Okay, let's get your coat and shirt off," she said once they'd gotten him seated on the exam table she'd thankfully just fitted with sheets and a blue paper cover. She and Zeke each carefully tugged at the wide sleeves of his coat and slipped it off, then unbuttoned his flannel shirt and did the same thing, exposing a fairly tight long-sleeved shirt beneath it.

"I hate to tell you this, but we're going to have to cut this shirt off. Trying to move your arm and shoulder enough to get it off over your head isn't a good idea. Okay?"

"Aw, man, I only have one duffel of clothes here to last me the year. But okay."

"I'll find scissors and get that done, Dr. Flynn," Zeke said. "And don't worry, Pete, we can always get more clothes sent here. It just takes some patience before it arrives." With quick, efficient movements, he had the shirt off in mere moments, which surprised Jordan. Trained medic or not, it wasn't what he did for a living, and she couldn't imagine he dealt with medical emergencies very often in his line of work.

Slowly, she moved her hands along Pete's arm, elbow and up to his shoulder, and when the man gasped and uttered a sharp cry, her eyes lifted to meet Zeke's.

"Dislocation, probably, don't you think?" Zeke said.

Just looking at it, she'd suspected the same thing, but her physical exam pretty much confirmed it, and she nodded. "Most likely. Which isn't fun, but better than a break. I'll get the portable X-ray to be sure. Is your arm numb or tingling, Pete? Can you move it?"

"Can hardly move it. And yeah, numb, and it hurts. A lot."

"How much pain, on a scale of one to ten, with ten being the worst?"

"I think an eight. Or nine." Pete grimaced.

"Okay. Be right back." She rolled the X-ray machine over to take the pictures, with Zeke coming up behind her to study the computer screen over her shoulder. He seemed big and unnerving, the scent of him in her nose and the sound of his soft breathing in her ear. Disgusted with herself, she shook off thinking about how close he was, the hyperawareness of him that seemed to happen every time he was near. She called on her training to study the images and think about her patient and nothing else.

"Definitely a dislocation, with just slight damage to your glenohumeral ligament. That's the ball and socket between your scapula and humerus—your shoulder bone and the top of your arm. See?" She pointed to the X-ray. "I'm going to do a reduction to pop it back into place again."

"Will that fix it?" Pete asked.

"It'll be tender for a while, and you'll need to wear a sling to protect it and help the ligaments heal. And yes, it'll fix it but you'll have to be careful not to injure it again. I'm going to give you a muscle relaxant, and an analgesic for the pain, so the reduction won't hurt too badly."

"How about I find those drugs for you?" Zeke asked.

"That would be great. Except they're still in a jumble in the box. I had them perfectly organized until that crazy earthquake while crossing the Drake Passage tossed them around, along with me. So you'll have to look for them."

Zeke's brown eyes met hers. The twinkle and warmth in them showed he was remembering everything about that night, too, and all of it made her belly feel a little funny as she smiled back.

"There was an earthquake? While we were on the ship?" Pete asked, his eyes wide.

"No, no." Jordan's face felt a little warm, realizing she was dangerously close to flirting with Zeke, which she absolutely did not want to do. Especially since she enjoyed it too much. "Just a joke between me and Dr. Edwards."

"Dr. Flynn seems to be accident-prone like you, Pete. Hopefully, not when she's reducing your shoulder, though."

"He's joking about that, too, Pete." She frowned at Zeke. Kidding around patients was good to a point, to help them relax, but not if the kidding made them worry that she didn't know what she was doing.

Thankfully, Pete didn't look horrified, chuckling instead. Jordan asked him for his personal information and filled out paperwork on the station's hospital computer. She continued making notes regarding her diagnosis, X-ray results and treatment plan, while Zeke brought the medications and water so Pete could take the pills, and was glad he'd come with her to help.

With the meds now having had enough time to take effect, she stood next to the patient and firmly grasped his arm and shoulder, preparing to do the necessary reduction to put it back in place. "Ready? This is going to hurt some."

Zeke reached to hold Pete's hand. "Hang on to me and squeeze. It'll help you get through it."

Pete nodded and pressed his lips together, and Jordan could tell he was gripping Zeke's hand so tightly it had to be uncomfortable. She concentrated on manipulating Pete's arm to reconnect it into his shoulder socket. After a long moment of maneuvering it around, she heard the satisfying *thunk* and felt it lock back into place. "There! That wasn't too bad, was it?" She stepped back to smile at her patient.

He huffed out a long breath. "Not gonna lie—it hurt. But it feels a lot better now."

"Good. Now I need to get you a sling, so sit still until we get your arm immobilized. I'll—"

"I grabbed one when I was back in the storage closet," Zeke interrupted, holding it up. "I'll put it on him."

He didn't even wait for her to respond, efficiently getting Pete's arm and shoulder set up in the sling. She opened her mouth to comment on the way it should be done, then closed it. Obviously, he knew exactly what to do. Obviously also liked being in charge, even when he wasn't. But she wasn't about to complain, because it had definitely been better for Pete, and for her, to have Zeke there with them, helping get the procedure done as efficiently as possible.

With nothing to do at that moment, she found herself distracted by Zeke's dark lashes fanning his cheeks as he concentrated on fastening the sling. At the focus in his brown eyes, interrupted with flashes of humor as he'd say something to Pete that made him laugh.

The man was too charming for his own good—or for hers—and eye candy, to boot. She didn't want any distractions from her work or her diving device trial, and wasn't about to get tempted by a guy who was not at all what she wanted for her future. Seductive brown eyes and a teasing, sexy smile didn't change that reality.

"Pete, I want you to come back the day after tomorrow so we can talk about how you're doing. Here's more of that pain reliever, with my instructions." She scribbled on a notepad, then handed it to him with the medication. "And sorry, but no snowmobile training, or anything else physical that uses your arm or shoulder, for at least two weeks. I suggest you rest for a while before you try to get back to work today."

"Will do. Thanks."

After another nod to Jordan and a shake of Zeke's hand, Pete was gone, leaving Jordan alone with Zeke. Their eyes met again, and the sizzle between them was disturbingly obvious. To cover her awareness of it, and of him, she turned to strip the blue paper from the exam table and tossed it in the trash. Before she moved to put away the equipment, she paused and gave him a deliberately impassive look, hoping to squelch the electric zing she could swear she physically felt crackling in the air around them.

"You…you have an excellent bedside manner," she managed to say, hoping to break the mesmerizing connection. "I'm impressed that you didn't even flinch when he squeezed your hand so tight I thought he might cut off your circulation."

"I've dealt with a lot of injuries in the field over the years. Offering a hand to someone in pain is the least I can do."

"I assume you'll be going back to the snowmobile practice?" she said.

"Nah. It'll be almost over by now, and there are other people to help the newbies if they need it."

He just stood there looking at her, his hands in his pockets, rocking back on his heels a little, and her silly heart sped up all over again at something in his expression she couldn't quite define, leaving her feeling breathless.

"Well, if you'll excuse me, I need to get to work. I have to organize all the things that are still a mess before more crew members get here, because as soon as they get settled in, I'll be recruiting some of the scientists to try my parents' earplug design for equalizing pressure during dives. Then schedule some dive time with them."

His brows practically hit his hairline. "What? What do you mean?"

The shock on his face made her realize she should have told him about the earplugs before, since he'd be diving a lot for his work here. Why hadn't she, when that was a big part of the reason she'd come to Antarctica? The obvious truth hit her. Feeling this constant push/pull of attraction every time he was near, and not wanting to feel that way, had knocked all thoughts of recruiting him straight from her brain.

"My parents have designed a device they hope will eliminate, or greatly reduce, problems with barotrauma. I'm an experienced diver and I'll be testing it here, and asking for volunteers to be part of the trial." She licked her lips and made herself ask the question she knew would result in them spending a lot more time together if he agreed. "Do you… Are you interested in being part of the trial, and diving with me sometimes?"

CHAPTER FOUR

ZEKE STARED AT HER, stunned. If she'd told him she wasn't really a surgeon at all he wouldn't have been more surprised. "You're a diver?"

"Yes. It's my parents' hobby. Their passion, really, after medicine. I told you that both worked as doctors in international hospitals, and I grew up diving with them all over the world. My dad studied biomedical engineering before deciding on med school, and he's sort of an amateur inventor. My mother loves to do underwater photography, has even sold some photos to magazines. I tried to dabble in that, but don't seem to have her artist's eye for it."

It took him a moment to respond, still astounded that in all their conversations about his work she hadn't said a thing about being a diver herself. "What is this device they invented?"

"Earplugs that equalize underwater pressure on the ear canal, without the diver having to clear their ears manually. They've just begun testing it various places. When I got this chance to come work in Antarctica, we all thought it would be a great opportunity to see if there are any differences in the way they perform in extremely cold waters."

"And you need volunteers to wear them. But why would you be diving, too?"

"Obviously, working in the clinic and hospital, I'd only be able to come along on dives occasionally. But I want to do that to record divers' thoughts right away, take their vital signs when possible and...okay, I admit it." A small smile played on her lips as her beautiful eyes met his. "I can't wait to see what it's like under the ice. Excited and scared, both, to be honest."

"Scared? Why?"

"You know as well as anyone that it's got to be different diving beneath ice than in the Caribbean. Isn't it?"

"It is." And he suddenly knew that, more than anything, he wanted to be the one diving with Jordan for her first time here, making sure she felt safe. "I'd be happy to be part of your trial. The rest of the marine biologists will be coming on the next boat. How about I talk with them about your trial as soon as they get here? And you and I can plan on a dive as soon as we can make it happen."

"Sounds perfect. I should have known that you'd dive right in…ha-ha—" she sent him an adorable smile "—and take over to help make it happen. And you know what? I'm getting rid of that independent streak you've scolded me about to tell you I really appreciate it. Having you be part of the trial and talk with your colleagues about it is going to be hugely helpful."

The smile on her face and the way she was looking at him seemed to show she felt sincerely pleased, and his chest felt like it was expanding as he thought about how good it would feel to help her. About how it would feel to spend more time with her and dive with her. Then he forced himself to remember that he couldn't let himself get attached to Jordan, that he'd be there for her when it came to working and diving, but anything more was out of the question.

He couldn't deny that the attraction he felt for her seemed to grow every time he saw her. But how he felt didn't matter. She might not be interested in a relationship, anyway, but if she was, she deserved someone she could rely on in every way.

He definitely wasn't that man.

Zeke doubled down to get everything ready for when the rest of the crew arrived so he and Jordan could get diving as soon as possible. He and some of the station crew spent the entire day out on the ice shelf, using chain saws, drills and heating equipment to cut two dive holes about twelve meters apart. Having them finished left him feeling satisfied and excited about getting down there to see what they'd find this trip, and to see how Jordan felt about diving under the ice.

His prediction? She'd love it, and he was counting the hours until the next ship would arrive with the other scientists, so he could get busy with his grant work and go underwater with her.

With the dive holes ready, he finished the aquarium setup and tested it to make sure it was operating properly. He checked the filter systems he'd had up and running for the past twenty-four hours, then the water quality. Pleased that all systems were go, he knew the other marine biologists would be glad he'd come early to get this done. Once they were diving, they'd bring back algae, zooplankton and other marine life samples to test, study and, in some cases, tag and return to the sea.

He forced himself to do paperwork so he'd have it behind him when everyone arrived. The ship should have left Chile an hour ago, which meant only two more days until he'd have dive partners as anxious as he was to get in the water.

Revision of his most recent academic paper, soon to be published in a science periodical, was the first priority. That study was complete, and an important piece of the complex data he'd be presenting to get his new grant application finished.

His current research project would take the full five months he'd be down here, but initial data had to be compiled in time for the first grant deadline, which was in just less than a month. For every grant available there were at least ten applicants, and getting the fieldwork done, the initial data compiled and the preliminary paper finished by early November would take hard work and a lot of hours.

Being one of the first to submit the application was critical. As a presenter at next year's international climate summit, he needed to have additional, irrefutable evidence of how the ozone hole above the Antarctic would continue to affect coastal cities and its inhabitants. Proving ways to reduce the amount of ice melt and disturbing water temperature rise, which was affecting the size and impact of hurricanes and typhoons, was what his life's work was all about.

He knew, firsthand, that people were dying because of it. Many more, if he failed.

Zeke drew in a deep breath. He'd get it done. Then he'd knock the socks off various nations' leaders and private enterprises interested in making corporate changes, and the global impact of all that would save lives around the world.

His grandfather's laughing face, his grandmother's sweet one, floated in his mind's eye, and with the ache and guilt came a familiar feeling of determination. He made a call to the vehicle coordinator to make sure they had a PistenBully or one of the six-wheel vans available to get to the ice shelf the day his colleagues showed up, so he could start pulling samples. Then he worked on more paperwork until his eyes were blurring.

"Might want to cancel your reservation for transportation," Bob Shamansky said as he strode into the room. "Looks like both of us are going to have to find more lab- and paperwork to do for a while."

"What? Why?"

"Just heard that John Stewart notified the base supervisor that he's keeping the tub docked in Chile because of the weather. Forty-knot storm on Drake Passage right now, and with the ship full, he doesn't want to risk it. Planning to wait a couple days and see if it calms down."

"Damn." Zeke pressed his palms to the table, trying to figure out how to get rolling on fieldwork without waiting another four or five days. "Maybe you can be my dive partner. Just to be ready to throw me a line if something happens."

"Pretty sure you need someone who can actually dive with you, in case you get the bends or a tear in your hose or whatever the hell can happen down there. Those things being why I don't participate in that particular activity."

"Yeah." Diving alone wasn't a great idea under normal circumstances, and here in Antarctica? Doing that would qualify as just plain stupid. "I'm going to see if anybody who's already here is a diver."

Except he already knew of one. Jordan Flynn. Would she be interested in diving with just him? Thinking about the excitement in her eyes when she'd spoken about it, he had a feeling the answer was a clear *yes*.

"Might be," Bob said. "Don't worry. If I know you, you'll get that grant money done come hell or high water." He clapped Zeke on the shoulder. "Time for first-round lunch. Why don't you go to the galley and ask around to see if there's a diver you don't know?"

"It's worth a try." Without much hope that he'd get lucky and find someone, he headed to the galley and, as expected, struck out. Feeling too restless to go back to his paperwork, he decided to see if Jordan was willing to dive with just him, and if she was, find out when she could take the time to do it. And it wasn't just an excuse to see her. He needed to get to work on gathering samples.

Though he couldn't lie to himself—the thought of seeing her did make his step feel a little lighter, whether he wanted it to or not.

He found her in the storage room of the clinic, sitting on the floor with her legs crossed. Bags of medicines and medical supplies were sorted in front of her, next to multiple zippered satchels, her head tipped forward, a waterfall of smooth hair covering her profile. He knew how soft it felt from when he'd glued her wound and now stood there a moment, wishing he had an excuse to skim his hand down all that dark silk.

He cleared his throat. "I wanted to talk with you, but looks like you're busy."

Her head lifted and her eyes met his, her fingers pushing her hair behind her ear as she smiled up at him. "No, just getting travel bags ready. Which I'm sure you know all about."

"What are you packing?"

"Drugs, syringes and other equipment, labeling each bag. Catheter. Fluid. Trauma. Circulation. IV. The usual."

"The usual for Antarctica. I'm impressed that a hospital-based surgeon knows everything you might need down here for out in the field."

"Well, much as I like to impress people whenever possible, I can't lie. I was given a list when I was hired, before I even came down here." She held up a sheaf of papers with a cute self-deprecating smile on her face. "Want to take a look and see if anything's missing?"

He lowered himself to sit next to her and liked the way his shoulder felt pressed against hers as he leaned in to read it. "Looks pretty complete to me. You're ready to go if there's an accident or illness in the field, Dr. Flynn."

"Good. I was a little worried that I hadn't finished this yet, so I'm glad to get it done."

"I'm glad, too. Because I came to talk to you about your work schedule and diving."

She began to push to her feet, and he regretted no longer getting to sit so close to

her, oddly comfortable considering how hard the floor was. He stood and held out his hand to finish helping her up, taking as long as possible to release her hand's warmth. She didn't seem in too big a hurry, either, looking up at him expectantly until she finally slid her hand from his.

"Do you have a dive scheduled with the new crew that I can come on?"

"Not exactly. Drake Passage is acting up again, and nobody's getting here for a few days. I don't want to get behind on gathering the samples I need for my grant application so I'm wondering—are you willing to dive with me alone?"

"Well, let me think." She tapped her finger against her chin. "You've been diving in Antarctica during thirteen trips and I doubt if anyone coming can beat that. So, is that a real question?"

"Wasn't sure if you'd feel safer as part of a bigger group, since you haven't been under the ice before."

"I know I'll feel totally safe with you," she said. The eyes meeting his were serious and trusting, and a strange feeling filled

his chest that she seemed to truly feel those ways about him.

"We won't wander too far from the hole, and stick close together. And whenever you're ready to go back up, just let me know and we'll finish right away."

"When can we go?"

"Does tomorrow afternoon work for you? Bob Shamansky said he'd come with us whenever I get a dive pulled together, and I know he won't be free until about three o'clock. He doesn't dive, but whenever we go out, we have at least one tender along to help with all the equipment and keep an eye out up above."

"An eye out? For what?"

"Marine mammals, among other things. Most are fun to see, like the penguins and the various seals, though you'll notice that some of the male seals glare at you if you get too close. Especially underwater, so give them a wide berth if you can."

"Sounds amazing."

"It is. Except there is one thing you have to steer clear of—leopard seals. They're dangerous, and if we see any in the water we move on and keep our distance."

"Do they attack people?"

"Sometimes, and even follow divers occasionally, like the predators they are. They have sharklike teeth and are huge. Males are about a thousand pounds and females even bigger. A few years ago, an intern was badly mauled by one at a station south of here. Just one more reason why diving here isn't like diving other places."

"Being mauled by a leopard seal sounds about as appealing as hypothermia," Jordan said, and her captivating smile showed him why he'd felt so attracted to her that very first day on the ship when she'd joked about that. "Which do you think would be worse?"

"Probably a toss-up. And I don't want to experience either one to find out the answer." But experiencing diving with the smart and fascinating Jordan Flynn? That he couldn't wait to do. "Can you be ready tomorrow at three in the vehicle hangar? I'll have all the equipment we need for when you and Bob get there."

"I brought my dive clothes and equipment, but I'm not completely sure I won't need something more. Do you have extra gear required for this kind of water?"

"Is that a real question?" For some reason, he couldn't help but tease her. "Yes. And I'm sure you're also prepared. All you have to do is wear what you'd normally wear when it's twenty degrees below Fahrenheit."

"Pretty sure there's no 'normal' in that kind of water temperature. Except here." Amused blue eyes met his. "Are you willing to try the earplugs?"

"Looking forward to it." And he was, but not nearly as much as he looked forward to diving with her, and wished they could head out right then.

"I appreciate that. So—"

Voices from the lobby outside had them both turning their heads, and the deep stab of disappointment that he wouldn't get to banter with her alone anymore surprised him.

"Uh…" He drew in a breath, knowing he had to quell this desire for her, because there was no point. "I guess you have a patient you need to see?"

CHAPTER FIVE

Jordan glanced out through the door at the people filing into the meeting room, wondering how in the world she could have forgotten she had a group coming in for first-aid instruction.

Except she knew how. Something about Ezekiel Edwards seemed to make her forget everything except how much she enjoyed talking with him, and laughing with him, and looking into his deep, dark eyes, and she felt herself falling every time. A hardworking man dedicated to his job and who liked to help people. A man whose smile made her feel annoyingly gooey inside whether she wanted to or not.

"Um…" She glanced at her watch. "I actually have first-aid instruction scheduled. For crew members coming…right now. The first ten for two hours, then another ten after that."

"Ah, the first-aid lessons. Need a hand?"

"Wow, you must be really bored." Or could it be that he didn't want to end their time together any more than she did? Which wasn't something she should want. But she did, anyway, fool that she apparently was.

"Not bored. I just know from experience that teaching newbies how to stitch, and place IVs, isn't easy."

"Are you offering your arm to let them place the IV? That would be entertaining to watch."

Amused brown eyes met hers as he laughed. "I'm not quite that much of a masochist. With this many people, I just know that having two instructors makes it go faster."

"I'm sure that's true." Jordan hadn't actually taught nonmedical people how to do the things on her list, but didn't want to confess that. It sounded like Zeke had, and she felt a pang of disappointment that it was probably the reason he'd offered, and not because he found being with her fascinating, the way she'd unfortunately been feeling about spending time with him.

But she wasn't too proud to learn something professionally from him, was she? Even if it was medical related? "We're going to start with first-aid basics, like treating shock, how to stop bleeding and such. Then go to the stitching and IV placement. Sure you don't want to be the human practice dummy?"

"Not that big a dummy."

That twinkle in his brown eyes and crooked, engaging grin were irresistible, and she couldn't help but laugh. Standing there next to him in what should have been a normal, casual interaction between colleagues felt strangely intimate instead. Like they'd known each other a long time, and shared a closeness she shouldn't feel after knowing him a matter of days. Though she supposed the time they had spent together had been unusual, with him patching her up and working at a science station that currently had a comparatively skeleton crew. Not to mention that she needed him to help her get underwater, and test her parents' device.

She couldn't seem to help that her breath

felt a little shallow and her heart was doing that annoying pit-a-pat thing. Her brain knew very well that he was not at all the kind of man she wanted in her life, but her body hadn't seemed to catch up with that fact.

She drew a deep breath and tried to shake it off so he wouldn't suspect her unwitting reaction to him. Though she feared he already knew.

"Don't worry, Zeke. I brought a phlebotomy and venipuncture practice arm, so your flesh and blood are safe."

"And speaking of flesh and blood, can I check on yours?"

She nodded and he stepped close again, his wide palm cupping the back of her head as his other hand gently moved aside her hair to look at her scalp wound. He smelled so good, his own mix of the outdoors and a faint whiff of soap and of *him*, and she found herself wanting to lean into him. To feel his big body pressing against hers, the memory of which seemed imprinted in her brain from when he'd carried her to her bunk.

"It's an even more impressive rainbow of

colors, but the swelling is down. Looks like it's healing well."

"When I was a little girl I wanted to be a unicorn the worst way, so I guess I'll think of having a rainbow on my head as a positive."

He gave a soft laugh. "Maybe you'll find something equally colorful and fantastic when we dive."

"I can't wait to find out." The damned breathlessness wouldn't seem to go away, and she was glad to have the excuse of starting the first-aid class to put distance between them. "Thanks again for patching me up. Maybe during class I'll show everyone my head and we'll demonstrate closing and gluing a wound, too."

"Gluing takes more skill than stitching, when it comes to emergency field treatment, though some don't believe that." His voice was a warm rumble, and she wondered if he realized the hand behind her head had brought her to within an inch of his broad chest. *She* realized it the second he'd done it, because being so close had her heart beating fast and her hand lifting to press against his chest, barely resisting the urge to slide it up around his neck and close the small gap between them.

"I guess we'll stick with teaching stitching, then."

Their gazes met and held, his hot and alive. His strong jaw, covered with dark stubble, looked taut, and his wide shoulders blocked the view of the people coming into the lobby, creating the illusion that they were still alone. Suddenly wanting, more than anything, to rise up on her toes and kiss that tempting mouth of his, to wrap her arms around his neck, foggily trying to remind herself of all the reasons she shouldn't... But then he broke the mesmerizing connection. Dropped his hand from her head and stepped back.

His chest rose and fell. Noise from the other room got louder as more people arrived, talking and laughing, and still, neither of them moved. It felt like time had simply stopped as they stared at one another.

And then he turned away.

"Sounds like everyone's ready to learn the basics, Dr. Flynn."

She watched him walk out into the lobby, then managed to pull herself together to follow. Which was completely annoying, since she was the one teaching this class, and should have been the first in there, smiling and welcoming everyone. Time to get her act together and remember why she was here, which definitely wasn't to make goo-goo eyes at a man who made his living researching and traveling, and was not someone she wanted to get personally involved with.

She hurried into the meeting room and greeted the crew, hoping her expression was relaxed and professional. Half the group was already seated at the table, picking up and examining the medical items in front of them, while the rest were still standing and chatting.

Her hyperawareness of Zeke's tall form at the other end of the table was a distraction, but the interest the crew had in learning about the first-aid techniques made it easier to move her attention to teaching. Everyone there knew there might be times they were away from the station in the field and would need to know how to do basic emergency treatment, or an occasion when Jordan was in the field herself and someone would have to take over here at the Fletcher during an emergency. The two hours went by quickly, and the whole thing turned out to be fun, to Jordan's surprise.

A big part of what made it fun? Ezekiel Edwards. His joking had everyone laughing at the same time they were learning. The man was not only knowledgeable, he seemed to have that perfect balance of knowing how to teach while keeping everyone engaged.

Just like he'd been there when she'd needed her scalp repaired, he'd been here for this, too. A man you could count on whenever you needed to. Having him as a partner for this training made it much less stressful and a lot more enjoyable, and the next important step was to convince her body and not just her brain that they needed to keep it strictly professional.

"Last is stitching a wound," Jordan said to the group, holding up a needle and suture. "It's really just like sewing, except you need to stop the bleeding the way we've already discussed, then clean the wound as best you can before you close it."

"Remember this is a field technique, though, as there might be a better option if someone is injured here at the station," Zeke said, seated between two people who were riveted by his every word. "Either Dr. Flynn or I will have derma glue on hand, which often can be used in place of stitching for smaller wounds. Especially scalp injuries, should your head make contact with a wall, or something."

He sent her that teasing smile of his, and the secret little connection between the two of them about what had happened the first night they'd met made her belly feel all fluttery. Their eyes met, and she just couldn't help but smile back, everyone else in the room seeming to fade into the background except for him.

She drew a breath and managed to turn away and focus on the crew. Ezekiel Edwards might be beyond appealing, but he was not irresistible. She could dive with him, and work with him, and still keep her heart firmly to herself. Work colleagues and simple friendship would be the goal.

The six-wheel van lumbered across the ice shelf, and Zeke hoped like hell that the dive would go smoothly without any kind of hitch. Having only two divers and one tender wasn't the norm down here, but he'd done it before. So why did he feel this niggle of worry?

The answer was obvious. He wanted today's dive to be a special experience for Jordan.

He glanced across the seat at her and wondered if the hum between the two of them as they drove was palpable even to Bob, who sat in the back seat. Then Zeke wondered if maybe it was all one-sided and he was imagining the connection between them. A connection, if it was real, that he shouldn't encourage, anyway.

"I can't believe how incredible it is out here," Jordan said, turning to look at him. The awe on her face made him smile, though he'd known all along she was the kind of person who would appreciate this crazy southern world of intense blue sky; barren, snow-covered mountains and the slow ice melt over beautiful blue-green waters as much as he did.

"It is incredible. The way it changes from day to day, even hour to hour sometimes, is like nothing you've seen before." He worked to keep his voice even and not warm and intimate, the way he couldn't seem to help feeling toward her ever since they'd packed up in the hangar earlier. Since yesterday, working together in the clinic. Since the moment they'd met. "Wait until the hours-long sunsets. Crazy storms. And, if you're lucky, the aurora australis—though that might not happen during your trip here. Once it's twenty-four-hour daylight, in another week or so, it'll be too late, and I don't know how much solar activity there's been lately to make them visible."

"I so hope I get to see it. But even if that doesn't happen, just being here is so much more amazing than I ever dreamed."

He took in her shining, excited eyes and wide smile as she scanned the expanse of white in the clear air, the iceberg chunks floating far out in the water, the Adélie penguins waddling along in groups of over a hundred, and hoped she'd be just as pleased once they were actually diving.

"Was it you who placed all these flags along where we're driving?" she asked. "I assume they mark the route?"

"Yeah," Bob chimed in from the back

seat. "Zeke and I spent a day getting the markers placed before he and a few burly engineer types came back to cut the dive holes. A couple trips ago, I learned how important it is, believe me."

"What happened?"

"We were at a small station with a group that got the holes placed, but didn't post flags. A nasty storm blew up and we couldn't see a thing. Barely made it back. I thought for sure we were goners, our bodies about to be buried under the snow before being eaten by a leopard seal."

"Bob is a little melodramatic, as you can tell. I always get the flags in first, so stop trying to scare her." Zeke sent a frown back to Bob, not wanting him to worry Jordan. It was true that getting lost in a blizzard was no joke, and preparation was critical.

Also true that no matter where you were, Antarctica or anywhere else, if you didn't plan for the worst-case scenario it could result in a tragedy you would never forget.

Zeke's chest tightened, and he battled back the familiar and unwelcome anxiety that would come from nowhere and that was beginning to well in his chest. Slow, calming breaths, in and out, usually pushed it away now, and he breathed and focused on the white road in front of him.

"How much farther to the dive hole?"

He turned to look at her, and seeing her beautiful face smiling and calm managed to help him relax, too. "See that speck of red in the distance? That's a tent set on top of the closest hole we cut. As we get deeper into the summer we can usually do without the tent and leave it open. This early in the season, though, it helps protect us from cold wind and snow as we're getting in and out of the water."

"I admit it's amazing to me that you dive here at all."

"Are you feeling nervous about it?" He reached for her hand, wanting to show he was there for her. "You don't have to go in. With both you and Bob as tenders, I'd be fine, especially if I stay fairly close to the hole."

"No, I want to experience it. Test the earplugs. But I've heard people feel claustrophobic under the ice sometimes. A little worried about that, to be honest."

"I don't want you to worry." He tightened his hold on her hand, and when she twined her fingers with his, his chest felt that strange expansion thing again. Hopefully, her holding on to him meant that she trusted him. "It's not that common with experienced divers, which you are. But if it happens to you, just like in any other dive situation, it's important not to panic. We'll attach a rope to your weight belt, so if you get weirded out, you know you can always follow it back up."

"I won't need a rope."

"Do you always try to act so big and tough and overconfident?" His heart jerked, wondering if she was going to pay attention to everything he said, or feel a need to show her independent self. If she did, he'd end the dive early, period. "Most divers here use ropes every time they go out, especially during midsummer, when the phytoplankton bloom and the water's murky. It's easy to be exploring and getting samples and not realize how far you've gone until you can't figure out where, or what direction, the hole is. That's when people freak, and bad stuff can happen."

"I promised you I'd stay close to you, didn't I?"

"You did. And I want you to keep that promise."

"I promise I'll keep my promise."

She said the words in a light joking tone, and gifted him with a smile that stole his breath. He squeezed her hand before he had to let it go, stopping the vehicle next to the tent.

"Here we are. Ready?"

"Ready or not, here I come."

"I haven't been a tender on one of these trips for a while, Zeke, so you'll have to remind me what to do with the equipment," Bob said.

"Okay." Since the whole reason they were here was to dive and get work started, and they needed a tender to do that, Zeke shouldn't feel slightly resentful of Bob's presence. He couldn't seem to help that he did a little, anyway, wishing he and Jordan could enjoy being here together all alone, even though that made no sense at all. "I'll explain as we get it set up by the dive hole."

Zeke shoved open his door and went to the back of the van, with Jordan and Bob following. After getting everything inside the tent, he turned to Jordan to talk with her about what was necessary for cold-water diving, because it was crucially important she understood how different it was from whatever diving she'd done before.

"Getting the gear on right matters. First, the dry suit goes on over your long underwear, then a jumpsuit on top of that. So, let's get it on you before we go to the next step."

She took off her snowsuit, boots and thick pants, folding and stacking them in a pile on the ice, and Zeke couldn't seem to keep from staring at her. He'd been on dozens and dozens of dives and never once had he thought of anything but work when everyone got their gear on, until today. That she could look so sexy in black long underwear that closely fitted her slender body had him imagining what she'd look like in scanty undies.

Or nothing at all.

Nearly groaning at the vision, he yanked his mind from where it had instantly gone, and held the dry suit open for her. "Step in, and I'll help you get it on."

"Remember I've dived many times in my

life?" She reached for it instead of doing as he asked. "I know how to get on a wet suit."

"Except this is a dry suit, and they're even tighter so you stay well-insulated in the water. But suit yourself. Literally."

"I always do," she said with a grin.

He tried, again, to think only professional thoughts as he watched the way she shoved her feet into the tight legs, tugging them up her delectable body an inch at a time. Wiggling and wriggling. Huffing and puffing, until he and Bob both couldn't control laughing just a little at her struggles.

"Another reason I don't dive," Bob said. "Way too much work before you even get in the water!"

"Well, sometimes it takes a little work to have a lot of fun," she replied, sounding breathless from her exertion.

"Very true." Zeke worked to get his on, too, but since he had the technique down pat, he'd already fastened his closed while hers was still twisted around her hips. "At this rate, the sun will be setting by the time you're ready," he said, cocking his head at her. "You going to let me help you or not?"

"Fine." She threw up her arms, sounding

exasperated. "But what happens on the ice stays on the ice, right? I don't want anyone knowing I couldn't do this on my own."

"It's our secret. And next time, you won't have as much trouble, I'm sure."

"While you finish, I'll get the last tanks from the van," Bob said before he disappeared from the tent.

Barely acknowledging Bob's words, Zeke looked down into amused blue eyes. He loved that Jordan could poke fun at herself, despite that independent streak of hers that didn't like asking for help with a dry suit she wasn't familiar with. He reached for where the suit was currently squeezing her hips, curled his fingers inside the rubber clinging to her body and tugged it upward, feeling her firm waist and ribs as he did. Her eyes lifted to his again, and his breath backed up in his lungs.

Being alone with her in this tent, touching her body and standing so close he could hear her breathing, was doing all kinds of things to him that he couldn't let happen. His gaze moved across the delicate shape of her face, her parted lips, her eyes staring up at him, and all he wanted to do was pull her into his arms and kiss her until neither of them could think.

He nearly did. He began to lower his face to hers, then gritted his teeth against the desire for her that pumped through his veins. He squeezed his eyes for a moment to block out how beautiful she was and the hot thoughts he had to control.

When he opened his eyes again, he focused on the dry suit as he tugged it up her body, making sure he didn't touch places he shouldn't touch, which wasn't easy. Finally, he got it high enough for her to stick her arms inside, and expelled a breath of relief that he'd survived it without doing something they'd both regret.

"That feel okay? Not crooked?"

"No, it's okay."

She sounded breathless, but probably from the exertion of getting the suit on, and not for the reasons he felt that way. He moved around to her back and took her soft hair into one hand to move it aside as he got the Velcro fastened around her neck. It felt like torture that he couldn't lean in a little closer to breathe in the scent of her skin. Press his mouth to her nape and taste it.

God, he needed to get out of this tent and into the water.

"There." He cleared his throat and stepped back. "You're in, but there's more."

She turned to face him, and something about her expression made him grit his teeth all over again, wanting more than anything to reach for her and kiss her and to hell with any consequences.

"The face masks. I've never worn one before."

"Yeah. They have that special perfume smell called eau de rubber. You'll like it."

Her laughter helped ease the uncomfortable closeness he kept feeling for her, standing alone and so close inside this tent, and he breathed a little easier.

"Eau de rubber sounds like it might become my new favorite," she said, and he didn't think he was imagining that she looked a little relieved to be back to their joking.

"I think this is everything, but you need to double-check, Zeke," Bob said, coming back inside.

"Looks like it. Except for one thing. Where

are the earplugs you want to test, Jordan?"
he asked.

"Right here." She reached for a small bag
inside a pocket of her folded snowsuit, and
pulled out four small black things, handing
him two. "I want you to put them in without
me instructing you how. To see if you think
they're user-friendly."

"Okay." Shaped a little like a music ear-
bud, he easily settled it down into his ear
canal. "There. I'd say definitely easy to put
in. Looking forward to seeing how they
work."

Her pleased smile in response to that
seemed to sneak right inside his chest,
warming him despite the chill in the tent. He
turned away to grab the hoods, face masks
and dry gloves, putting his on to show her
how. Focusing on her midsection and getting
the rest of the equipment on her didn't help
dull the desire he couldn't seem to control,
which seemed impossible, since she was
covered head to toe with black rubber that
obscured every inch of her skin except the
little bit he could still see until she put her
goggles on, and her lips.

"Weight belts next, then the buoyancy

compensator vest, goggles, regulators and tanks."

His gaze met hers, gleaming blue from inside the black mask, and he nearly told her she was the only person he'd ever dived with that he wanted to kiss while literally covered head to toe in rubber.

He was in so much trouble here.

"Here's when I finally admit it." Her eyes were filled with rueful laughter. "I thought I'd researched most of what I needed to learn to dive here. But I sure didn't know I'd feel like a human tire, complete with inner tube and snow chains. Not sure I can even walk the five feet to the dive hole."

"Consider it weight and cardio training." He handed her the regulator and needed to make sure she knew how diving here was different from what she'd done before. "Remember that regulators are more prone to get stuck in this kind of cold, so pay attention to that. Don't get stressed about it, just replace it with your spare if it does. If your hands get cold, which they probably will, hold them above your head for a couple minutes. The warm air from inside your suit will rise into your fingers."

"Interesting. Okay."

"We're not going to stay in a long time for your first dive, so you can see what it's like. Are you ready?"

"Ready as I'll ever be."

"Bob will be at the other end of the rope up top, so if you get worried, you can follow it and tug hard if you want Bob to help pull you back to the hole."

"Want me to tie it?" Bob asked, holding it up.

"No, thanks. I'll tie it to one of the loops at the back of the suit." The slight prick of fear that something could go wrong and she'd suffer because of it stabbed at him, and he wanted to be the one to ensure the rope was tied correctly. It was a little obsessive, and he knew it, but he couldn't help but check three times to make sure the rope was attached to her good and tight.

"You want to go in first, or follow me?"

"I guess I'll go first."

"You sure?" Most divers new to Antarctica wanted to follow, but he shouldn't have been surprised. Jordan Flynn obviously was the kind of woman who refused to let herself be intimidated, or if she was, she dealt with it head-on.

"I'm sure."

He watched as she waddled to the dive hole, smiling at the way she stiffened her shoulders at the edge as she looked down into the water. Standing there and taking a long pause to mentally ready herself like most people? Not Jordan. Three seconds later, she plunged in and he followed.

CHAPTER SIX

THE MAGIC OF underwater Antarctica never failed to thrill Zeke, no matter how many times he'd dived here. Gathering samples could wait until he saw how Jordan adjusted to this dark and amazing world. His chest feeling a little tight, he watched her, wondering if it might bother her to be under the ice. She pointed at the hundreds of red and pink starfish strewn across the ocean floor, the sea urchins and coral and brightly colored fish, her eyes looking at him with obvious delight, and the tightness eased.

He reached for her hand, partly because he wanted to hold it, and partly because it calmed the slight tension he couldn't seem to help feeling as they swam together. He showed her more of the amazing marine life, from beautiful to strange to the algae and small creatures he collected for his work.

It struck him that he hadn't felt a need to clear his ears, and realized the earplugs must actually be doing what they'd been designed to do. Jordan would be happy to hear that, and he sent her a thumbs-up. She sent one back, though she couldn't have known why he'd done it, and they smiled at one another through the darkly shimmering water as they explored.

Wandering around like sightseers, enjoying her curiosity and pleasure, weren't the reasons they were down here, though, and he reluctantly released her hand to leave her on her own, but not far away. He tucked the samples he collected into the bag attached to his waist while trying to keep an eye on her as she swam around.

He smiled at her excited gesturing when several Weddell seals swam close, looking at them curiously. A hole in the ice fairly close by, not large enough for humans but big enough for seals to slide through, was doubtless where they'd entered the water, and he pointed to it. She nodded, her smile obvious even behind the regulator between her teeth.

A buoyant feeling lifted him, and it wasn't the water, it was Jordan. Had he ever enjoyed seeing someone dive for the first time here as much as he was enjoying her obvious delight? The pleasure of being with her in the magical waters of the Antarctic made him forget how long they'd been down there until he realized his fingers felt cold, and knew hers were probably even colder.

He pointed upward, and she nodded and followed him for the five or so minutes it took to swim back to the dive hole. Getting out of the water and onto the ice was the hardest part of diving, with the weight of all the equipment, and he shoved her rear end from below. Hopefully, she wouldn't think he was using the situation as an excuse to touch her. Or know how much he wanted to.

Her flippers thrashed a few times before she disappeared, then he followed, heaving himself up to sit on the side of the hole. He shoved his mask up to see her lying prone on her back, her mask shoved off and her regulator loose on the ice, a wide smile on her face even as she sucked in air.

"I'm guessing you liked it?"

"Oh, my God." She turned that beautiful blue gaze to him. "*Liked* isn't even close to the word. That was…unbelievable. So much more amazing than I'd ever dreamed. The colors! I thought it might be too dark to see much sea life but…wow! The creatures! The blue! The light! I'm…speechless."

"Not quite speechless." He chuckled, and that buoyant feeling filled his chest again, though he knew that was a little ridiculous. She'd come to Antarctica on her own, to work and dive, and she'd have done it without him. Still, he couldn't help but feel lucky that he'd been the one to introduce this special world to her.

"You're making me feel like I need to learn to dive, too," Bob said.

"You should. It's…it's…"

"Unbelievable? Amazing?"

"Yes. And a lot more."

"Go ahead and lay there for a minute and catch your breath, warm up a little," Zeke said. "Bob and I will help you with your gear after I get mine off."

Jordan sat up, and he lifted the heavy tanks from her shoulders as she shrugged them off into his hands. Bob carried them and some of the other gear to the back of the van, and Zeke grabbed a small towel to dry Jordan's hair and face.

"Helps you warm up faster if you're dry." Looking into her eyes, he wiped down all visible skin, then watched her squeeze her hair with the towel. It nearly had him forgetting they were just dive partners, not lovers. He barely stopped himself from leaning in for the kiss he'd wanted all day.

"Thanks for...warming me up. Got to admit, I was starting to feel a little numb."

He lifted his hand to slowly wipe another trickle of water from her cheek as they stared at one another, both wearing small smiles.

"Oh, I almost forgot. I need to take your vitals after wearing the ear devices. Do you feel like they worked?"

"You know, I do. Pressure pain isn't something that affects me very often, but I didn't have to clear my ears at all. I'll use them every time I dive, and see if it's any different next time. But go ahead and take my vitals."

"Should have done it the second you got

out of the water, but I was thinking about… other things." She quickly turned to pull a stethoscope from her bag with an abrupt motion that made him wonder if the "other things" might have been exactly what he'd been thinking about since the second they'd come on this excursion.

She stared straight at his chest as she pressed the stethoscope against it, her brows lowered in concentration. "Your respiratory rate is slightly elevated, as is your heart rate, but that's to be expected."

"Yes, I would expect that to be the case."

Her expression told him she might have guessed from the tone of his voice exactly what he meant, which had nothing to do with diving and everything to do with her standing so close and touching him, but she apparently decided not to comment on it.

"I'll get your gear, too, Zeke," Bob said as he ducked back into the tent.

"Thanks. Appreciate it."

Bob's arrival forced Zeke to rip his gaze and his mind off Jordan's body as she peeled the wet suit off her torso and down to her waist. The thin underlayer of clothing slowly being exposed were molded to her gentle curves, and it struck him all over again.

Jordan Flynn's body was pretty much perfect.

Zeke turned away to gather more equipment, and his equilibrium, as Jordan finished getting her gear off and her regular clothes back on. He huffed out a sigh of relief, even as he wondered why the hell the sight of her wearing what were in essence long johns seemed incredibly tempting and beyond sexy.

The cold air on his face as he ducked out of the tent helped cool his thoughts, and he packed the tanks in the car, with Bob and Jordan showing up a minute later with more gear. With the last of it stowed, Zeke shut the back doors of the van and the three of them got into the vehicle and headed back to the station.

Jordan talked enthusiastically to Bob about the dive, enough that Zeke didn't feel a need to chime in. The chatter let him pay attention to the route across the ice, or at least as much as he could, considering his hyperawareness of Jordan sitting only a few feet away. He couldn't seem to keep from glancing over to look at her, even as he told himself not to.

Her smooth skin was pink from the cold. Her dark hair was in wavy disarray, and he wanted to run his fingers through it and mess it up even more. Thoughts of kissing her breathless as he held her face in his hands invaded his brain all over again, and if she'd taken his vital signs again right that minute, she'd have found his heart rate elevated and his respiratory rate high again just from thinking about her. Which was absurd, he knew, but he couldn't seem to control the insistent desire for her that had taken over all his common sense.

Somehow, those thoughts had to stop, but he had a bad feeling that the only solution was to stop spending time with her. Something he didn't want to do. Which was a quandary he wasn't sure how to fix.

Bob's satellite phone rang in his pocket and Zeke saw in the rearview mirror that the other man was frowning as he listened. Then he looked up at Jordan. "Okay. I'll tell her. We just left. We're about an hour away from Fletcher, right, Zeke?"

"About that. What's wrong?"

"Is someone injured?" Jordan asked.

"Sick. Not sure what's wrong, but he's out at one of the temporary field stations. Apparently felt bad the past two days, but now he's worse. The person with him says there's no way he's capable of traveling behind the Ski-Doo."

"Did they say what his symptoms are?"

"Confusion. Fatigue. Irregular heart rate." Bob leaned forward. "I guess the guy with him wanted to bring him to Fletcher's clinic as soon as he heard you were here and had it open, but the man who felt sick was sure he just had a bug. And now he can hardly walk."

Jordan grabbed her field bag from the storage closet, hoping she hadn't missed anything she needed. Good thing she'd finished putting it all together before she'd let herself be distracted and interrupted by a certain sexy marine biologist/climatologist.

The whole time they'd been together in the van, in the tent and even in the water that certain something had simmered between them, hot and alive, whether she wanted it to or not. Her brain kept trying to remind her that he was not the kind of man she wanted a relationship with, and that she wasn't a fling kind of woman, but it seemed the rest of her wasn't listening too well.

Professionally? It was good for them to spend time together. He'd needed to get diving, and she'd wanted to start the earplug trial, not to mention that diving here had been the most glorious experience of her life.

Was there any way for her to benefit from their professional relationship, diving and exploring Antarctica, without falling deeper under Ezekiel Edwards's spell?

She had no idea, which felt a little scary. And now, here they were again, with no choice but to be working together, and physically close, on this field expedition. She couldn't go alone to see the patient, and it made no sense to ask someone else to join her when Zeke was the only other person currently at the station who had any kind of medical experience. He also had significant field experience, driving the snow machines across areas that might easily have crevasses and other hazards. She had to admit that having him take the lead on this trek, instead of someone she didn't know, made her feel more comfortable, safer, when it came to venturing into the Antarctic wilderness.

"I brought my field kit, too, just to see if there's something in here we'd need in addition to your supplies," Zeke said as he strode into the clinic. "The crew attached a stretcher to the sled behind the Ski-Doo, so we have what we need if we have to bring him back."

She looked up and paused in shrugging on the backpack she'd stuffed full of supplies, unexpectedly riveted by the way he looked, dressed ruggedly for this trip. How could he seem somehow bigger, tougher, even sexier, than when she'd left him only half an hour ago? Apparently, she was becoming more idiotic by the minute when it came to Ezekiel Edwards.

She heaved in a breath. "Ready when you are."

"You have thick gloves and hat? A balaclava you can cover your mouth with? It's going to be a long, cold ride."

"It's all shoved in my pockets." Much as she wanted to see more of this amazing, white world, she couldn't claim to be excited about traveling out in the cold for over an hour. Though she'd better get used to it, since she was going to be working here for months.

"Let's get going, then. Your chariot awaits."

She turned away from the magnetic power of his smile. She led the way out of the clinic, conscious of him following close behind, both surprised and impressed, damn it, that he wasn't immediately telling her which hallways and stairways they needed to go down to get to the hangar. Her usual good sense of direction was finally kicking in, and in a short time they'd arrived to see the snow machines were all ready to go. Obviously, the crew all were aware that time could be critical when they had no idea how sick the patient might be.

She looked up at Zeke after he'd tied their packs to the machines and checked the stretcher ropes. "Can we ride them? Or do we have to do the skiing-behind thing?"

"Skiing behind, I'm sorry to say. Not as much fun for you, I know." He flashed that knee-weakening smile. "But since you didn't get to practice the technique, you can just stand behind it while I hit the throttle for you, instead of doing it solo. It'll be faster, and with less risk of our all-important doctor wiping out the way Pete did."

"Are you surprised that I'm not going to complain about that?"

"No, because you're a smart woman." He handed her the skis. "Put these on, then take the ropes in your hands. I've already got them tied tight. After you get going, I'll catch up and take the lead."

"Got it."

"I'll be keeping an eye out on the landscape, looking for cracks that could mean a crevasse. But like I said before, sometimes they're covered with blowing snow, and you're in one before you know it. If that happens, remember what to do?"

"Let the ropes go."

"Right. We never like to lose a Ski-Doo, but better than a lost life." His smile was long gone, his dark eyes serious as they met hers.

"Should we separate out the medical gear onto both the machines, so we still have enough to check on the patient in case that should happen?"

"Obviously, you're a natural for working on the ice, thinking about things like that." His grim expression lightened. "Losing a machine and equipment doesn't happen often, but I have my first-aid bag on my machine, in case we need it. Not as much as you have, but enough."

Zeke Edwards may be a scientist and medic, not a doctor, but his carefully thought-out plans for this trip, as well as their earlier dive, showed he knew exactly what he was doing no matter which career hat he was wearing. She'd learned a fair amount about medical preparedness from her parents' work in developing nations, but it was clear he had a lot more knowledge about emergency situations outside a controlled environment like a hospital than she did.

"Give me a thumbs-up when you've got the ropes in hand and are ready," he said as he stood to the side of her machine. "And if you ever feel worried about something, or just get tired and want to stop and take a break, give me a thumbs-down and I'll get it turned off."

"Thanks, but I think I'll be fine. I mean,

it's pulling me so not much exertion on my part, right?"

"We might hit some snow that's frozen into waves, which will make for a bumpy ride. If we do, that's pretty damned tiring, so don't try to be all tough, as I've seen you like to be, Dr. Flynn." His dark gaze met hers, held, before he gently tapped her nose with his gloved finger, moved it down to stroke her cheek, then tugged her balaclava up to cover everything but her eyes. "Taking a short break isn't a weakness, it means we'll be ready to do the work we need to do when we get there."

She nodded and held her breath as he reached for the throttle, hoping she didn't fall flat on her face, and gave the thumbs-up. The machine roared to a start, then began to move—slowly enough that she felt totally in control, thank heavens, her skis sliding across the crystalline, brilliant white landscape.

She couldn't see behind her, but heard his machine start, too, and in a short time he was beside her. His mouth was hidden behind a balaclava, but the smile in his eyes as they met hers was clear, and she couldn't help but smile, too. What a wild feeling to be pulled along, crossing this spectacular frozen desert that looked like nothing else on Earth.

Zeke's Ski-Doo moved to the lead, and stayed there for a long time. Jordan had no idea how long, but he'd been right—the machine doing all the work didn't mean it wasn't hard, but the beauty of the landscape made it easy to ignore any discomfort. She noticed that he kept looking behind to see if she was there, and knowing he was keeping an eye on her helped her feel confident that they'd get there in one piece.

Eventually, he slowed his speed to match hers and they rode side by side, with him turning to tilt his head at her, a questioning look in his eyes, every ten minutes or so. When she'd respond with a thumbs-up, he'd send her a fist pump, sometimes releasing his handlebars for an enthusiastic double pump that made her chuckle.

By the time they got to the field camp, which she was surprised to see was just two tents set up next to one another, Jordan's arms were stiff and tired. But the exhilarating ride had been worth every ache, and she was glad they'd made good time to see what was going on with their patient.

Zeke stopped his machine, then ran to stop hers, too. He pulled his balaclava down beneath his chin, revealing a wide smile. He moved in close, his thigh pressing against her leg as he leaned in to grasp her thickly gloved hands with his. "You did absolutely great. Feeling okay?"

"Good. Okay, my arms hurt a little and my legs feel slightly numb, but wow. I loved it! Just incredible."

"I fell in love with Antarctica the first time I came here, and still love it today. You're a woman after my own heart."

Her own heart gave a little jerk, then thumped harder at the expression on his face. Sincere and admiring, and the attraction that kept simmering between them, no matter how she felt about it, hung in the cold air. Something that felt alive and electric and oh-so-warm. Her gaze dropped to his lips, mere inches from hers. Would they feel cold against hers? Or had they stayed warm behind that cloth? Maybe sharing one little kiss with him wouldn't be a big deal...

"Thank God you're here!"

They both turned to the voice. A man with a thick beard emerged from one of the tents, a deeply worried expression on his face.

Time to forget about all that zing between her and Zeke that she still wasn't sure how to deal with, and get to work.

She dismounted the snow machine and held out her hand. "I'm Dr. Jordan Flynn. And this is Dr. Zeke Edwards, who's a marine biologist but also a field medic."

"Dave Crabtree. Really appreciate you coming out here."

"I assume the patient is in one of these tents?"

"Yes. He's been in a lot of pain, and having trouble moving his arms and legs. Then he got sick to his stomach, but kept saying he was sure it was just a bug that would pass. When he started acting confused earlier today and his legs seemed weaker than ever, I knew he needed to be seen by a doc, but also knew there was no way to get him to Fletcher's hospital without a stretcher here to pull him on."

"That's what we're here for." She turned to Zeke. "Let's get the supply bags, then check him out."

"I'll get them. You go on in."

Yet again, Zeke was proving what a great partner he was in these kinds of situations, fine with being her backup instead of wanting to see the patient at the same time she did to offer his opinions. She followed Dave, ducking into the tent behind him. There was barely enough room for the three of them, and it would be even more crowded once Zeke came in, but that couldn't be helped.

The patient lay inside a sleeping bag, his eyelids flickering open as she came to kneel next to him.

"I'm Dr. Flynn. What's your name?"

He didn't respond for a moment, which was alarming. Finally, he replied, "Jim Reynolds. Thanks…for coming."

"Tell me what's going on."

"My muscles feel…strange. Hurt. My arms and legs especially. Can hardly move them. Got sick to my stomach a couple times."

"When did you first start to feel this way?"

"Uh, I think…yesterday morning."

"Okay. I'm going to take your vital signs." She looked up at Zeke, who'd just come inside the tent but already had the field bags open and was handing her a stethoscope. "Can you find the oxygen saturation monitor?"

"Right here." Zeke clipped it to the patient's fingertip as Jordan listened to his lungs, then had Jim hold a thermometer under his tongue while she felt his pulse.

"Your heart rate is elevated." She frowned, because it was surprisingly fast. "Can you get me the blood pressure cuff, please?"

Zeke already had it in his hand and held it out to her. "Want me to put it around his arm and get the reading?"

"Yes, thanks. I'm going to check his pulse again." Maybe she'd gotten it wrong the first time, but no. Still far faster than it should be.

"Blood pressure is low," Zeke said, his eyes meeting hers, and she nodded.

"Let me see the thermometer now, Jim," she said, sliding it from beneath his tongue. Significantly febrile, and she held it up to show Zeke, then the results of the oxygen saturation, which was also elevated.

Their eyes met again. The combination of symptoms and test results weren't close to giving her a clinical diagnosis. She definitely needed to ask more questions to see if his answers would provide more clues.

"Tell me about your last few days here, Jim. You came by snow machine?"

"Yeah. Got here pretty early. Spent the afternoon climbing up to get some ice core samples until it got dark about ten."

"That was a damn tiring day," Dave added. "We both felt wiped out. Then the next day we took the machines to a high glacier farther out, and did some more climbing and core collection."

"So, a lot of exertion in a pretty short period of time. How long have you been in Antarctica?"

"Got here early this week."

"Probably on the same boat we did," Zeke murmured.

Sounded likely. She looked up at Zeke and nodded before turning back to the patient. "Tell me about your stomach pain. Are your bowels working? Does your urine seem normal?"

"Yeah." Jim's brows lowered as he seemed to think. "Actually, urine is really dark. Figured I'm a little dehydrated. Thought that might be why my stomach was hurting, too, but when I started throwing up, I realized it must be a bug. Been drinking water to get better hydrated and flush out whatever was making me sick."

"Have you been drinking alcohol, as well? More than normal?"

"Well, yeah. I have." His lips twisted. "Been hitting the bourbon to help me sleep. My back's been hurting like hell, and keeping me awake, and it's not easy to sleep in these tents, anyway."

"I see. I think I know what's probably going on, Jim." She looked up at Zeke again, a feeling of triumph filling her chest as the likely diagnosis now seemed clear. "Rhabdomyolysis. Extreme exertion compared to what he's used to doing at home. Dehydration. Excess alcohol contributing."

"Rhabdo?" Zeke raised his brows, then smiled and gave her a nodding salute. "That's one quick diagnosis, Doctor, but I bet you're absolutely right. I never would have figured that out."

"You might have, with more questions and testing."

"Nope. My field skills are good when it comes to injuries, heart attack and stroke—

but rhabdo? That's out of my wheelhouse. Congratulations."

The warmth and admiration in his words put a little glow in her chest, which was ridiculous. As though she deserved credit for coming up with a diagnosis most any other doctor would have been able to figure out. But coming from Zeke, it seemed to mean something more than a simple compliment.

"So, now what?" Dave asked.

"We insert an IV line in to push fluids. Give him some analgesics to help with his pain, then get him to the hospital at Fletcher Station to continue with the fluids and keep him under observation for a couple days."

"Can't I just stay here with the IV in for a day or so?"

"Rhabdo is no joke, Jim. It's not something you can just let ride its course. Liver or kidney damage can occur if you're not carefully monitored."

"Here's the IV," Zeke said. "I'll get the bag of fluids ready to go."

Jordan shoved up Jim's sleeve, cleaned the skin and got the IV placed in his arm. Zeke attached the bag of fluid, placed the analgesic pills on Jim's tongue and tipped a water bottle into his mouth to help him swallow, then stood.

"Glad you figured out the rhabdo, and we have what we need to push fluids. But we do have a problem," Zeke said.

She looked up at him, surprised at how serious he looked. "What's that?"

"No way can we get him back to Fletcher tonight."

"What? Why not?"

"Sun sets tonight at ten p.m. and it's now nine. It's not safe to drive the Ski-Doos when it's dark, or even in very low light, because you can't keep an eye out for cracks. We'll have to stay here for the night, and take him back in the morning."

Jordan realized her mouth was hanging open as she stared at him, and forced it shut, her heart beating in her throat. "You mean, the four of us cram into these two tents?"

"No Antarctic explorer goes anywhere without a tent and sleeping bags, in case a storm moves in. Or it gets dark. Or some other emergency arises, like this, where we had to come right away even though it was getting late when we left."

"A tent? As in one?" Her voice came out in a little gasp.

"One tent. A tight squeeze for two people, I admit. But I'm sure you knew life could get tough sometimes working at the south pole." He stood and his grim expression showed he wasn't any happier about the situation than she was. "I guess this is one of those times, and we'll just have to deal with it."

CHAPTER SEVEN

WITH THE WIND kicking powdery gusts of snow into their faces, Zeke aimed the head-lamp attached to his forehead at the tent, trying to get it set up as quickly as possible so Jordan could get out of the cold air. She hadn't uttered a word of complaint. But what he could see of her face beneath her bala-clava, bandanna and hat as she helped him pound stakes into the ice showed her eyes were watering, and she kept slapping her mittens together to warm her hands.

The look of horror on her face when he'd told her they'd have to share this tent would have been almost comical, if he hadn't shared the same damn concern. The chem-istry shimmering between them all day couldn't be denied. But he didn't do relationships, and it was pretty clear that she didn't want to go there, either.

The two of them being in extremely close quarters for the night was going to tax his already shaky self-control, and she probably knew that. But he couldn't and wouldn't make love with Jordan, even if she wanted to, because he wasn't the kind of man she deserved. Being close to someone, caring about someone, wasn't something he wanted in his life. Not ever.

He had to give her credit, though. Once the initial shock had passed, she'd been completely calm and professional, immediately jumping in to help with their gear and set up the tent. Working together made the process go as fast as possible, even with the low visibility they had to deal with.

"That's about it," he said, tying down a corner. "Go ahead and get inside, so you can warm up. I just have a couple little things to finish."

"Not fair for you to be out here doing the work alone. What's left?"

He glanced at her pinched face, her nose and cheeks the color of a scarlet sea star, and had to admire the hell out of her. He'd worked with countless people during his many Antarctic expeditions, and plenty—both men and women—had been happy to duck out of cold wind when given the chance.

"I appreciate the offer. But—"

"Zeke!" She pointed behind him and her face lit with wonder. "Is that…? Oh, my gosh, that has to be the aurora australis!"

He turned and, sure enough, the night sky was lit with ribbons of green light, curling to meet luminous, salmon-pink waves, rising like a shimmering wall from the horizon to the stars. "Well, damn. You get to see it, after all, and that one's a beauty. You must have brought some serious good luck," he said, so glad she was getting to see this incredible phenomenon that everyone coming down here wanted to experience, but rarely did after September. "Last two times I came in the summer I didn't get to see it at all. Nothing like it, is there?"

"It's…unbelievable," she breathed, her expression rapt as she stared. "I hardly dared to hope I'd get to see it, since it's going to be twenty-four hours of sun in, what? Three or four days?"

"Something like that." He finished the last tent tie, then switched off his headlamp. The darkness fell around them as the green and pink ribbons undulated across the sky. He moved to stand behind her, resting his hands on her shoulders. "I always feel like the luckiest guy on Earth when this happens. It's like being in another universe, don't you think? Or acting in a movie with special effects, but this is real. Electrons, atoms and molecules colliding with the Earth's magnetic core. Wonders all around us, creating a spectacle like none other."

"The photos I've seen are beautiful, but this? Actually seeing it? More stunning than I could even imagine."

The heavenly display seemed to envelop them, wrap around them, making Zeke feel as though they were strangely cocooned together, alone in the universe, and he held her with her back close against his chest. His arms moved to circle her waist, trying to shield her from the biting wind as they watched the colors swirl across the sky, both of them silent for a long time.

Problem was, neither of them were as bundled as they needed to be, since they'd only planned to be out here as long as it took to set up the tent. As minutes passed, the raw, frigid air began to seep through his gloves and layers of clothes, and he knew she had to be feeling it, too.

It struck him that standing beneath this celestial wonder, sharing it with Jordan, was something he'd never forget. He hated for the moment to end, but knew staying out here any longer wasn't a good idea. Regret weighed in his chest, knowing he'd never experience anything like this again. He lowered his head and pressed his cheek to her temple, and even through the layers felt her warmth.

"I hate to say it, but probably we should go inside and warm up away from this wind. Our bodies will put off more heat than you'd think, and fill the tent space pretty well, but if we get too cold, it'll be hard to get comfortable again."

She turned in his arms, and the look of wonder and awe and joy on her face had him holding her a little tighter, feeling beyond blessed that they'd seen the wonder of the lights together. "I appreciate you staying out here with me. For keeping me as warm as you could, so I could soak in that incredible sight. It's something I'll never forget. Thank you."

"No thanks necessary." The words came out gruff, his throat a little tight that she would thank him for holding her close in the cold Antarctic air. God knew he'd done it both to keep her warm, and because folding her into his arms was something he'd wanted for days, and now had experienced for real. "I feel lucky every time I get to see it. And getting to share it with someone seeing the lights for the first time? That feels... good."

"The word *good* is not even close to what I'm feeling right now."

Something about the way she said it, combined with the way she was looking at him, sent his heart beating a little harder, his breath a little short. He couldn't help but let his gaze lower to her lips, pink from the cold, wanting to kiss her even more than he'd wanted to earlier, which seemed impossible. Then she leaned into him, grasped his shoulders in her hands, moved them to his cheeks. Tipped her face up to his and had a look in her eyes that told him she was thinking about that first night they met. How it had felt when he'd held her in his arms. All the times since that he hadn't been able to stop thinking about it, either.

She rose onto her toes, and with a soft groan, he took the invitation. Lowered his mouth to touch hers. Moved across the sweetness of her cold lips. Let his tongue slip inside her warm mouth, tasting and exploring, going deeper, and a gasp of obvious pleasure left her mouth and swirled into his.

"Zeke." She said it in a way that showed him she was feeling every bit as aroused as he was. He could feel the thin string of control he'd tried to maintain snap as he gave in to the desire filling his chest and stirring his body. He held her close, pulling her hard against him, wishing they weren't both wearing heavy snowsuits and gloves that restricted his ability to feel the curves and heat of her body. He kissed her until he lost all sense of time and place, thinking of nothing but how perfect she felt in his arms. How she tasted even better than he'd imagined, and how he wanted more. And more. And more.

A strong gust of wind blew across them, creating a snow devil that swirled up from the ground, spattering tiny shards of ice against the exposed skin of their faces, finally forcing them to pull apart. Breathing hard, they stared at one another until the snow had them squinting against it, and ducking their heads to protect themselves.

"Let's get inside," he said, grasping her arm and leading her to the small round opening in the tent, barely visible through the snow churning in the darkness. "Go in headfirst. I'll get the sleeping bags, then follow you."

He switched his headlamp back on, found the gear they needed to sleep comfortably for the night, then squeezed into the tent. "Here's a flashlight in case you need it," he said, handing it to her. "Your sleeping bag and an extra blanket."

"What about my other things?"

He looked up at her as he unrolled his sleeping bag onto the cold tent floor. "What do you need?"

"My eye mask and white-noise machine," she said with an impish smile.

"Well, damn. Why didn't I remember those for a wilderness roughing-it trip?" He loved her sense of humor, and had to laugh.

Loved spending time with her, period. "Do you really use those all the time?"

"All the time. I told you I lived different places around the world as a kid, going wherever my parents worked. Believe me, those two things help you sleep no matter where you are."

"Your parents are doctors, you said. So why did they travel so much?"

"They work for an organization that sends medical teams to places lacking health care. It also responds when there are disasters like earthquakes and hurricanes."

"I…admire that. Those things are often a whole lot worse than anyone can tell from TV clips. The numbers they give about injured and killed don't tell the story. Every person affected is loved by someone." His throat closed at the memories, and since he didn't want her to see anything on his face that might make her ask questions, he busied himself getting some of the supplies set out, including a water jug.

"Drink some," he said, handing it to her. "You already know, Dr. Flynn, that in extreme cold, dehydration is a big issue." He watched her as she took a deep drink, her tongue licking a few drops from her lips. Memories of what they'd just shared outside tempted him to lean over and kiss her wet mouth all over again.

Maybe she saw a gleam in his eye, because she turned away, and he tried to think of that as a good thing, even though it didn't feel like it. She scooted down into her sleeping bag. Her gaze met his, and damn if all the humor had left her eyes, replaced by a serious look. "So, about the kissing. I admit it was incredibly special out under the lights and I… I really enjoyed it." She gave a small laugh. "A lot. Which I'm sure you noticed. I like you. I like spending time with you. But it's not a good idea."

"Getting to kiss you under the southern lights is about as good as anything will ever get in this world." Zeke reached to cup her face in his palm, and the way she pressed her cheek against it was at odds with what she'd just said. "But you're right. Anything more than friendship between us isn't a good idea."

"I have to admit I'm totally surprised you just said that. But I'm glad you're not mad at me."

"I'm not mad at you." He wasn't going to tell her why he felt that way, but wanted to know why she did. If it wasn't him, what was it? Had some guy hurt her?

He slid into his sleeping bag and looked at her, enjoying the intimate feeling of their faces being so close to one another, of being able to see the little dark flecks in her beautiful eyes. He wasn't sure what to do, or not to do. But talking seemed like a good first step.

"Since you don't dislike me, and I've agreed that our getting involved isn't something we want to do, tell me about you. Do you not do relationships?" If that was the case, she'd be more like him than he ever would have expected.

"It's not important," she said, staring up at the top of the tent. Her voice sounded a little forlorn, and he knew that talking about things from your past that still bothered you was always cathartic. Not that he ever did. He didn't like to go back in time and face failures and think about how things could have been different any more than he had to. But getting Jordan to confide whatever it was that was bothering her, then hopefully feel better about it, felt important.

He reached over and stroked her hair. Would have held her hand, except her head was the only part of her outside the sleeping bag. "I'm a good listener. And you can count on me to keep whatever you tell me just between us."

"Some of it's silly. I mean, it goes all the way back to being a little girl and how I felt when we'd go visit my grandparents and cousins maybe once every few years."

"Feelings are never silly," he said quietly. "We feel what we feel. So tell me about little-girl Jordan."

She sighed and turned her head to look at him again. "Part of me knows I had a special childhood. Living so many places and being exposed to so many cultures taught me a lot and shaped me in a way most kids don't get shaped, you know? But there was a huge negative that came with never having roots anywhere. No place I could really call home."

"I understand roots. They can be an important part of your life. Sometimes the most important part."

"I wouldn't know. So tell me about yours."

"We're talking about you." Touching her face again helped him shove down the familiar pain. "If you never experienced having a place to call home, what made you think you even wanted that?"

"I'd see my cousins, and how close they were, on those rare times we visited. Saw them playing with neighborhood friends, everybody knowing each other so well. I never felt like I fit in. I was the outsider, and wanted in so badly. After being there a couple weeks, I'd start to feel like I was getting there, maybe starting to be part of the family. Then we'd leave again."

"That would be hard for a kid." His own family had meant so much to him, and when he'd lost them, a part of who he was had gotten lost, too. "Did your parents know you felt that way?"

"I told them, and they tried to understand. When I was fourteen, they even offered to have me live with my grandparents for a year and experience the life I craved, but by then, my outsider status felt too entrenched, you know? I was… I hate to admit it, but I felt afraid that I'd never fit in and be stuck there and miserable, anyway. So I stayed with my parents and our gypsy lifestyle." She turned and gave him a half smile, obviously trying to lighten the mood. "Except we missed out on that whole gypsy-caravan thing—it was just us. And honestly, hearing myself talk, I sound ungrateful for all the good things my upbringing brought me."

Her eyes looked troubled, and the guilt he saw there tugged at his heart. "A person can appreciate things about their life and still wish it might have been different."

"I suppose. But anyway." Her voice brightened even more. "I went to medical school in the States, moved to England and fell in love with the place. I decided that was where I was going to put down the roots I never had. Have a good job, marry a nice man, live in a real house that belongs to us and have a small brood of kiddos. Like a normal person. Maybe that sounds boring to you, but it's what I want. It's what I've wanted forever."

"Doesn't sound boring." Again, he shoved down the memories of his own roots. His own family. "So, let me read between the lines. Wanting the whole husband-and-family-and-roots thing means a short-term affair with anyone who doesn't qualify as a potential mate isn't going to happen."

"You are remarkably astute."

Her smile was back, the real one that lit her face and made him smile, too, and he was glad that getting her to talk had turned out to be a good thing. He stroked her soft hair again, ran his fingertip down her cheek, because he needed to touch her. "I knew from the second I met you that you're a special woman. Adventurous, courageous, smart and damned beautiful on top of it all. You deserve everything you want in life. And you're right that I don't qualify. More than you know."

He leaned across the few inches between them and pressed his lips to her cheek. Slid them over her soft skin to give her lush mouth one last kiss, his heart squeezing that he couldn't be the kind of man she wanted. "Good night, Dr. Flynn. You should know that in the short time we've spent together, there are several things you've taught me. One just tonight."

"That I'm astonishingly conventional?"

"No." He swallowed, somehow forcing

humor into his voice that he suddenly wasn't feeling at all. "That I need to add eye masks to the emergency kits on the Ski-Doo. And invest in a battery-operated white-noise machine."

Her soft laughter sneaked into his chest and stayed there. It soothed the ache around his heart and warmed him until he fell asleep, the sound of her soft breathing in his ears better than any white-noise machine could ever be.

CHAPTER EIGHT

THE DRAKE PASSAGE had finally calmed and the boat would apparently be docking any second, which Jordan was glad about. She wanted to be busier, and she also wanted to get more divers to try the earplug device. Zeke had said he thought it worked, which was exciting, but she needed a lot of data, not just one man's opinion, from one dive.

Zeke. She didn't want to admit it to herself, but she missed seeing him. In the light of day, outside the intimate cocoon of that tent, she'd felt a little embarrassed at her confessions about her childhood longings that had formed what she'd decided she wanted for her adulthood.

But he'd been a wonderful listener, and his words in response had been supportive, not critical. Ever since they'd been back at

the station, he hadn't come to sit next to
her in the galley. Hadn't asked her to dive
with him again. She hadn't even caught him
watching her as she ate, the way she had the
first few days she'd been there, just sending
her a casual wave and a smile if they saw
one another across the room.

She should be glad about that. The com-
plication of a relationship with him here,
when there could be no future for them after
the expedition was over, wasn't worth it. The
way she'd reacted to his kisses, to his smiles,
to his touch, told her she could have fallen
way too hard for the man, and for what? Six
months of fun, followed by months of missing him? Or worse, meeting men at home
and feeling like they just didn't measure up?

She huffed out a long breath. That would
be terrible and she could absolutely see it
happening. In so many ways, Zeke Edwards
was larger than life, but he was *not* the
"forever after" she wanted. He'd even told
her as much. No, the future love of her life
was waiting somewhere for her in London,
and with any luck, she'd be meeting him
in the not-too-distant future after she left
Antarctica.

So why couldn't she get Ezekiel Edwards off her mind?

Practically every time she thought of the amazing aurora australis, memories of the seductive kiss they'd shared made her lips tingle and her mouth water. She'd thought of him during the next rounds of first-aid training, which he hadn't come to, even though last time he'd said he'd help again. She'd missed his teasing smile and amused eyes and the warmth he brought to every room the minute he walked in.

Fletcher Station was big enough that they rarely ran into each other, and yet she found herself looking for him wherever she went, hoping to see him. And that was just plain annoying. Ridiculous, when she'd been the one to tell him an ice affair was not on her list of things to do, and he'd fully agreed that he didn't want one, either. Thank heavens that, with so many new people arriving today, more work would provide the distraction she apparently needed.

She heaved a sigh and went to the hospital wing to check on Jim Reynolds, pleased to see how much better he looked than he had a few days ago in that tent when the rhabdomyolysis had left him temporarily paralyzed.

"How are you feeling? Good to see you've got some color back in your face," she said as she checked his pulse and listened to his lungs.

"I feel okay. Ready to go back to work."

"Your vital signs are all normal now, so I'm discharging you today. Which I'm sure you're glad about." She smiled. "But I want you to take it easy here at the station before you head into the field again. And when you do, don't try to climb and extract ice cores for hours on end. Be sure to pace yourself."

"I will, Dr. Flynn." He nodded. "Dave was just in here about ten minutes ago, and he said the next boat has already docked and everyone's on their way here. He's going to recruit more crew to come with us on our next trip to the mountains in a couple days, so we won't be working alone for nearly as many hours."

"Glad to hear that." She wrote out instructions for him, and made some notes into the computer. "I'll be back soon with your clothes, and medication that I want you to take for another week."

The distant ping of the satellite phone, which only worked a few hours a day, surprised her, and she hurried to the clinic office to answer it. Who could be calling? Her stomach tightened at the thought that it might be someone reporting another medical crisis to deal with in the field.

"Dr. Flynn."

"Hey, you! How's it going at the south pole for the amazing Jordan Flynn?"

The voice of her old med school roommate had her relaxing and smiling, and she realized she'd missed the kind of normal friends and normal conversations she took for granted at work back home. "Lia! How great to hear your voice. It's good down here. So beautiful, you almost can't believe it. It's been slow, work-wise, since the next boats were a few days late because of weather. But they're here now, so I'll be superbusy soon."

"I want pics when you can send some. Can't imagine you down there! Have you had a chance to test your parents' earplug thing yet?"

"I went on one dive, and tried them myself. And one other diver did, as well. Too small a sample, obviously, with uncertain results so far. I have to collect a lot more data, which I'll be getting soon now that more divers are here." She decided she wouldn't say anything about supersexy Zeke, because Lia would probably be shocked that she was attracted to someone here, and they weren't involved with each other, anyway. "Being underwater, seeing all the sea life, is mind-blowing."

"Diving down there sounds crazy to me, but you've always been an adventurer."

An adventurer. That had been true, from the way she'd grown up. But this probably would be her last adventure for a while. "Tell me about you. Are things…bad at home?"

"Yes. Worse than bad." Lia's voice turned angry, which was so unlike her. Jordan knew she must be facing a mess. "My father's still missing, but I know it's only because he doesn't want to be found. I have a private investigator on his tail, but so far no luck. No matter how much time and money it takes, I'm determined to find him. I didn't train to be a surgeon to stay here in my little Portuguese village and run it instead of working in medicine, just because he's abandoned everyone. But…anyway. I'll deal with it."

"I'm so sorry you're going through this." Poor Lia, having to step into her father's role at the family vineyard in Portugal. As if she hadn't had enough trouble and heartache after the big fire there, and her fiancé taking off and completely disappearing right before they were to get married. Everyone had seemed so happy, with all the plans for the wedding going so beautifully, and Jordan had been so pleased when Lia asked her to be her maid of honor. She never would have dreamed that Weston was apparently a huge jerk. "I know you probably couldn't get away, with all you have going on there, but if by chance you want a break from all that, there's a job posted for another doctor down here. If you're at all interested."

"Oh, I'd love to come work with you there, and see that place! I doubt I could make it happen, but it does sound interesting."

"I'll email you the link from the job board, so you can look at it. Meanwhile, I hope—"

Static suddenly filled the line, and after trying to reconnect with Lia for a few minutes, she gave up. The satellite phones here had a mind of their own, and having only short windows to talk with people, or receive

TV news from the world, was something she'd soon learned that everyone accepted as part of life in Antarctica.

She set the phone back down on the desk and wondered if Zeke ever talked to people back home. Family, or coworkers. Or old girlfriends.

There the man was, back in her brain again, and she smacked herself on the head, only to wince because her bruise wasn't fully healed. How long would it be before she stopped thinking about him twenty times a day?

She heard the outer door open, and went to see who it was. A man walked into the clinic with a young woman by his side and held out his hand with a smile. "You must be Jordan Flynn. I'm Tony Bradshaw, the medical director, as you might have guessed. This is Megan Mackie, the nurse who's going to be working with us. Sorry to be late getting here. Weather was dicey even when we were finally able to cross, but we made it."

"A little wild when I crossed, too," Jordan said. The smile she sent the two of them faltered a little as she remembered that crazy first night in her cabin. Her split-open head.

Being held in Zeke's arms. "Glad you're here now, though."

"Has it been hard working without help?"

"Only about seventy-five people came on the first boat with me, and once I got the medical center set up and the field bags done, I felt like I was looking for work, to be honest. Though getting baseline physicals has kept me fairly busy, and you probably remember I'm running a trial on earplugs designed to address barotrauma."

"I do remember that. I'll be interested to see how the trial turns out." He slowly ran his hand down his face and seemed to force another smile, and she wondered how tired the man might be after the long delay and the rough Drake Channel crossing they'd gone through.

She also had to wonder if he might have worked at a different Antarctic station over the winter, since the man was about as pale as a human could be. But now wasn't the time to ask personal questions. They'd be working together for months, and there'd be plenty of time to learn about the other two medical staff working with her.

"I'm so excited to be working in Antarctica," Megan said. "Just the drive from the ferry was unbelievable."

"It's an amazing place, that's for sure." She opened her mouth to share the utterly magical experience of seeing the aurora australis but then didn't, because she realized she didn't want to talk about it, wanting to hold the memory close to her heart instead.

Sharing that moment with Zeke had made it more special, more intimate, more incredible than if she'd experienced it with anyone else. Enveloped by that dark night sky filled with stars and ribbons of light that had seemed to bind them together. A feeling of closeness that had her reaching up to kiss him without thought about whether she should or shouldn't, because it had just felt right.

"I heard there's a party tonight," Megan said enthusiastically. "So everyone can get acquainted. Are you going?"

A party? Jordan's feeling of melancholy suddenly faded as she wondered if Zeke would be there. "I hadn't heard. When is it?"

"They announced it on the boat. At the galley, wherever that is. Tonight at seven. Games and a band and stuff. Sounds fun."

"I'll stop by to meet some of the new crew. It'll be a good opportunity to find new divers to be part of my trial." And an opportunity to see Zeke Edwards's handsome face again. There might not be any point in her wanting to, but she did, anyway. Even if it was just from across the room.

It seemed impossible that the somewhat sterile-looking galley had been transformed into something resembling a cross between a disco and a casino. Colored lights moved across a dance floor, and country music blasted from huge speakers flanking the band. Jordan scanned the room for Zeke and, when she didn't see him, scolded herself for the disappointment she felt.

This party was a chance to make new friends, not moon over Zeke when they'd both agreed to cool the heat and stop with the kisses. She forced herself to look at the other tables for people to sit with, and saw a smiling Megan surrounded by young men. The male to female ratio at Fletcher Station was heavily skewed, and a pretty young woman was guaranteed to get a lot of attention.

Jordan smiled, glad the nurse was obviously getting along just fine. She wandered to a long table covered with finger foods, put some on a plate and settled into a chair at a small round table. She watched people laughing and dancing and decided that, when she was done eating, she'd get out of her work rut and get up there, too. Not wanting an affair with someone down here didn't mean she couldn't have other kinds of fun, right?

A guy asked if she wanted to dance. When she turned to answer, her heart jolted as she saw a tall, eye-catching man walk in the door. He was smiling and joking with Bob Shamansky and several other men, and suddenly she found it hard to swallow her food as her breath caught in her throat.

Really, Jordan? Back to this?

But scolding herself didn't stop her heart from beating harder and her stomach from getting that silly fluttery feeling. She said something to answer the man about dancing but had no clue how she'd responded, her focus entirely on Zeke.

So much for getting over her unwitting fascination with the man.

As though he knew exactly where she was, his head turned and their eyes met. The inexplicable electricity between them seemed to spark all the way across the room, raising the hair on her arms and leaving her breathless.

He moved toward her with a slow, steady gait, and her heart seemed to beat harder with every step. They just looked at one another, and it felt strange and thrilling and Jordan had no idea what to do about this thing between them that they'd agreed they didn't want, except to ask him to sit with her and maybe she'd figure it out.

"Would you—"

"Is this seat taken?"

A sexy smile slowly spread across his face and she laughed a little nervously. "No. Not taken. Would you like to sit down?"

"Thank you." He lowered his long body into the chair and scooted it right next to hers. "It's a little loud in here. But the music is good, don't you think?"

"I'm not normally a country music fan, but I do like this band. Especially the lyrics."

"The one about crying in your beer? Or

the guy who chooses fishing over his girl-friend?"

"Hard to pick a favorite. Is there one about a scuba diver who chooses zooplankton over a woman? Maybe you should write that one."

She'd meant it as a joke to cover her nervousness, but the eyes looking into hers weren't laughing. "Believe me, if I was a different kind of man, I'd want both. The zooplankton, and a beautiful woman who liked to dive for it with me."

She could feel her pulse fluttering in her throat. The man staring at her with what looked like longing in his gaze didn't seem to be the same man she'd shared a tent with. The man who'd agreed that anything between them was a bad idea. This man seemed to be eating her up whole with his eyes, and she found herself leaning close, all words drying up in her throat.

His big hand curled around her arm, slid down to grasp hers. "Want to dance?"

CHAPTER NINE

NOT SURE WHAT would happen if she tried to speak again, Jordan simply nodded, and they moved to the dance floor. He wrapped one arm around her waist and tucked her close against him, breasts to chest, their gazes fused, and her hand snaked up to the back of his neck before she'd even realized it. The music seemed to beat a primal rhythm through her body and the connection between them felt so intense it was like nothing she'd ever experienced in her life.

Neither spoke, and it almost felt like a dream. A different kind of dream than being underwater with him, but a fantasy nonetheless. Colored lights skimmed across his face, illuminating the dips and planes, his sensual lips, his dark eyes, and as they moved slowly together, his cheek pressed to her temple and it felt almost as though they were one, completely alone among all the other dancers in the room.

When the music stopped, it felt like they parted in slow motion, and she swayed forward, feeling bereft as they just looked at one another.

"You want a drink?" he asked, his voice rough.

"I… Yes, please. A glass of wine."

He nodded and went to the bar that had been set up for the night. The line was fairly long, and Jordan figured she should sit down again, especially since her knees felt weak and wobbly. The band took a break, and someone turned on the television that was attached high on one of the galley's walls, which she now knew meant the satellite was working and they'd grab some news from the world outside Antarctica while they could.

Only half listening to the TV announcer, she tried to concentrate on the screen instead of a certain überhandsome marine biologist and her reaction to him and what, if anything, she was prepared to do about it. Maybe ruling out a fling with him had been an all-wrong decision, except he'd agreed it was wrong, hadn't he?

Except the man who'd held her in his arms tonight didn't seem to feel that way anymore, which was beyond confusing.

Deep in thought, she stared up at the television. Then the disturbing images caught her attention for real.

"Devastating flooding and wind speeds up to one hundred fifty miles an hour from the category five hurricane has destroyed countless homes in North and South Carolina, including many whose occupants had chosen not to evacuate. Uprooted trees and floodwaters have destroyed cars, bridges and roads, with some people taking refuge on their roofs. Helicopter crews have had to temporarily halt the rescue of survivors until the wind speeds have died down."

The images were horrible—homes blown away, cars floating down streets, boats smashed and awash on beaches and at marinas. She turned to look at Zeke, not even knowing why that was her first reaction to the terrible news. Maybe to see if he was watching the devastation. As a climatologist, hurricanes had to be part of his specialty, she knew, so he'd definitely want to know more about it.

Except his expression wasn't one of professional interest. He was standing now, staring at the screen, his hands fisted on a table. Maybe the lighting was creating an illusion, but it seemed his skin had turned a little gray, his eyes shadowed. His lips were pressed tightly together. He stood motionless as Bob Shamansky came to stand next to him, putting his hand on Zeke's shoulder and looking concerned as he spoke.

Zeke responded with a jerky nod, then, in a sudden movement, left the table to stride out the door with Bob watching him go.

Shocked that he'd left without a word to her, Jordan found herself walking over to Bob. She needed to know why Zeke had looked so upset, then had abruptly left without getting their drinks. Maybe he needed to record data about the storm for his work, but somehow she knew it was more than that.

"Bob. Is something wrong with Zeke? He seemed…upset."

Bob turned to her, his expression grim. "I'm not sure. But I'm guessing this kind of thing might bring back bad memories."

"Memories of what?"

"I know he grew up in New Orleans, and was visiting there when Hurricane Katrina hit. He's never said much, so I don't know how he might have been personally affected. Maybe he doesn't like to talk about it because the city was such a wreck afterward, with almost everyone displaced. Couldn't have felt good to have the place you grew up in destroyed like that."

So, hurricanes were personal to him, not just part of what he did for a living, wanting to slow the impact of climate change. Warmer ocean waters meant stronger hurricanes and more devastation. More lives lost. Had Katrina been part of the reason he'd gone into marine biology and climatology?

When she'd shared her story in the tent, he'd talked about roots being important. Perhaps having his uprooted from that storm was a memory he didn't like to be reminded of.

Should she reach out to him, if he was upset? Be there for him, the way he'd been there for her when she'd hit her head? When she'd needed his help diving, and going into the field to see Jim Reynolds?

Maybe he wouldn't welcome her if she went to talk to him. Maybe he just wanted to be alone. In fact, he probably did, or he would have come back to tell her he had to leave, right?

She pictured the way his face had looked just now and decided that, no matter what, she wanted to be there for him, as his friend, if nothing else. Inhaling a deep breath, she left the party.

She kept going down the hallway, realizing she had no idea where to find him. The first places to look would be the marine biology lab, his office and the aquarium.

But he wasn't in any of those places. She asked the few people she ran into if they'd seen him, or knew where he was, but got shrugs and shaking heads in response.

Maybe he'd gone to his cabin, wanting to be alone. And if he did, would it be pushy of her to go there?

She didn't know. God, she just didn't know. But what kind of friend wouldn't check on him, and find out if he was okay? A bad friend, that's what. And she cared about him, whatever the status of their relationship. So she was going to knock on his door, and if he told her to go away, she would.

That decision had her straightening her shoulders and moving forward. Problem was, she had another hurdle to jump. She knew he lived in Pod B, but had no idea which cabin was his. It took her ten minutes to find a roster listing names and numbers, and every minute of it had her feeling more anxious, though she reminded herself she might be completely overreacting. There had been quite a few bad hurricanes since Katrina, hadn't there? So probably she was imagining that the look she'd seen on his face was one of anguish.

Finally armed with his cabin number, she stood in front of it with her heart beating in her throat. She drew a fortifying breath before she knocked on the door. No answer. She knocked again. Chewed on her lip. Wondered where in the world he could be, and if maybe not finding him was a sign that her mission was a little absurd. Just as she was about to turn away, the door opened.

She looked up at him, his face now wiped clean of all the emotion she thought she'd seen there earlier, and the different emotion that had been there when they'd danced. Her tongue stuck to the roof of her mouth, and suddenly she had no idea what to say.

"Jordan. Damn, I'm sorry. I...forgot about your drink. I remembered I had some urgent work to do, but I should have said goodbye."

"That's okay, I just..." She swallowed and forged on, even though this now felt like a really misguided idea. "Can I come in?"

He stared down at her for a long moment before he silently opened the door wide. She glanced around the room, briefly sidetracked from her worries as she saw the beautiful photography on the walls. Pictures of colorful starfish and urchins like those she'd seen with him when they'd been underwater together. Photos of unusual fish, and all kinds of coral, and a lot of other things she couldn't name.

"Did you take these pictures?"

"For my work." He nodded. "Photographic samples to supplement the physical ones is part of the research. Important to include in the reports when I apply for a new grant. Which is what I'm working on now. Got to get it done and turned in next week."

"My mother would be impressed. Yours are…beautiful."

Her gaze moved to a small table identical to the one in her cabin. For the first time, she saw that his laptop was open, with some kind of spreadsheet on the screen, and various papers were stacked on either side. Warmth filled her cheeks as she realized he was simply working, not moping or upset, and she had made a fool of herself coming there. Except she deserved to know why one minute he'd been holding her close, and the next he'd practically run from the room, didn't she?

No. He didn't want a relationship with her, and her stupid mooning over him probably had her reading things into their dance together that hadn't been there at all.

"I'm…so sorry I interrupted you. I'll leave you to it."

She turned to go, beyond anxious to get out of there before he found out why she'd chased after him, but his fingers wrapped around her arm and stopped her.

"Tell me why you're here," he asked quietly. "Is it because I left you? I'm sorry. Sometimes work makes me do strange things, but I hope I didn't hurt your feelings."

Maybe he *had* hurt her feelings, but that wasn't why she was there. She stared up into his brown eyes, and couldn't read them. "No. I was just being silly."

"Silly how?"

Lord, he wasn't going to make this easy for her. She wasn't about to tell him how mesmerized and confused she'd felt during their dance. But probably she should confess that she'd thought, looking at him as he saw the hurricane footage, that he was upset. That she'd been concerned about him. Maybe she had to embarrass herself that way because, otherwise, he'd think she'd decided to chase after him after one simple dance, which would be even more embarrassing.

"I was horrified by the hurricane footage. I looked at you to see if you were watching, and I thought maybe you seemed upset. And then you left. So I asked Bob, and he told me…" She stopped. Thinking about it now, it seemed ridiculous that she'd have been worried just because Zeke had been in a bad hurricane once in his life.

"Told you what?"

She drew a deep breath, and realized there was no going back. "That you grew up in New Orleans. That you were visiting when Hurricane Katrina hit. That must have been...stressful."

He turned to stare out the small window, his back to her. When he didn't answer, she didn't know whether she should respect his privacy, or press for answers about what he'd experienced. To see if he needed comfort.

Suddenly, she felt like the biggest fool in the world, and couldn't wait to get out of there, away from whatever he must be thinking about her showing up at his cabin uninvited.

"Never mind. I'll just...go now."

He turned back, his expression grim. He closed the gap between them, took her hand and sat down on the single bed, tugging her to sit next to him, hip to hip.

"I might as well tell you. Which will prove to you that you have good instincts."

"What do you mean?"

"You knew from the minute we met that I wasn't someone you could ever count on."

"What do you mean?" she repeated. "I never said that. You *have* been a person I could count on. You fixed my head. Came diving with me even when you weren't sure you wanted to. Helped me with two different patients, not to mention that it would have been a struggle to find someone to go into the field with me to see Jim if you hadn't been around. You were there every time I needed you to be."

"That's different than what I'm talking about." He twined his fingers with hers and looked down at them. "It's true that I grew up in New Orleans. My parents died in a car accident when I was six, and my grandparents raised me there."

"Oh, Zeke. I'm so sorry."

"It was a long time ago, but even though I was so young, I still remember how strange it was to have them just…gone. How incredibly confusing and hard. The only thing that helped me get through it was my relationship with my grandparents. That comfort and stability when they took me in and gave me a home." He looked up at her, and her heart ached for him when she saw the deep sadness in his eyes. "I was going to college in San Diego, and went home to New Orleans for a few weeks, between semesters.

To see my grandparents and friends. Dive in the Gulf of Mexico, like I always had growing up. It's what made me want to go into marine biology, and sent me to Southern California to go to school."

"And you were in New Orleans when the hurricane hit."

"Yes, at my grandparents' house. It was a category three hurricane when it made landfall, not normally the worst. But the winds weren't what caused the devastation. With the city sitting lower than sea level, when the levee broke, the gulf waters just poured in. The flooding was like nothing any of us ever imagined. The water just kept rising, until it was six feet up the walls of the house and still coming. My grandparents wanted to make a raft of some kind with the lumber they had stacked in their garage that we could use to float out of there."

Her fingers tightened on his. "Did you?"

He slowly shook his head. "I didn't think it was a good idea. My grandfather didn't know how to swim, and the best my grandmother could do was a dog paddle. A raft would have taken time to build, time I wasn't sure we had. And I was afraid if the water got fast, or we hit a tree or whatever while we were floating on that surging water, they'd get knocked off and maybe drown. I'm a strong swimmer, but I didn't feel confident I could save them both. Plus, I didn't even know where the water was running to, and wanted to figure that out while I came up with a plan."

She stayed silent, listening, her heart cracking, a deep dread filling her stomach that this story might end with a tragedy.

A long minute went by before he continued. "I remembered where a rowboat had been tied to a fence, just a few blocks away. It wouldn't be easy to get there in the fast-moving flood, but I knew I could make it, and hoped like hell nobody else had used it. Figured that, on the way, I'd be able to study the different directions the water was flowing, then bring the boat back. Get them into it, which would be a lot safer than a rickety handmade raft, and easier to steer, too, because there were oars attached. So I told them to stay put on the second floor of the house. That I'd be right back."

"Oh, Zeke," she whispered. "What happened?"

"I was so glad to see that the boat was still there, and I rowed it back. It took a long time because the water was rising fast, scary fast, but I was sure that, with the boat, once I got there to pick them up, they'd be okay. The closer I got to the house, the more scared I felt, because I could see the water was way higher than when I'd first left. All the way up to the second floors of houses as I passed. I got there as fast as I could, rowing right up to the second-floor window and tying the boat to the drapes. Went through the window, and the water was up to my chest. I called and swam through the upstairs, but they weren't there."

"Oh, my God." She was afraid to ask where they'd gone, so she kept silent, dreading to hear the rest.

"I got back in the boat and went everywhere, calling for them. Picked up a few other people as I did, and took them to safety. Over the next few days, I kept looking for my grandparents. In the neighborhood, in shelters, followed miles of water and mud, everywhere I could think of. I thought they just didn't know how to reach me, you know? No cell phones. No power. I figured we'd eventually find each other."

"But you didn't." She didn't say it as a question. Because the answer was stark on his face.

"I looked for almost month. Wasn't going to go back to school until I'd found them. Then I finally did." His eyes lifted to hers. "They were in with the many unclaimed bodies in the morgue."

Tears thickened her throat and stung her eyes as she wrapped her arms around his body, but he stayed stiff within her embrace. "I'm so sorry. So very sorry. I can't even imagine what you went through."

"No, you can't. Because you're not a person who would have done what I did. You would have stayed with them, found a way out together. But what did I do? I left. I left them to die."

"Zeke." She leaned back, shocked that he would say such a thing, after his heroic efforts in the midst of a nightmare. "You did not leave them to die. You left them to get help. To find a way to get them out. You did the absolute best you could in a terrible situation."

"Obviously not true." He lifted his hands to cup her cheeks in his wide palms. "The reason I'll never have a relationship with a woman, the kind of relationship you're looking for, that you deserve, is because I didn't just lose my grandparents. I lost something inside myself. The minute I got back to San Diego, I broke it off with the girl I was dating, because I can't ever be close to someone again. I don't want to be."

"Zeke. The terrible trauma you went through isn't letting you see with clear vision. Your memories of that awful time are skewed. I know because, even in the short time I've known you, you've shown the kind of strength and character that anyone would admire. You didn't leave your grandparents to die. Do you think closing yourself off from ever being close to someone is something they'd want for you?"

"Doesn't matter. I can't feel things like that. Care about someone like that. Not anymore. Not ever again."

His eyes were shadowed with guilt and pain, and her heart squeezed hard in her chest for all he'd been through. Maybe there was nothing she could do to convince him that what she'd said was true. Perhaps all she could accomplish was to make him forget, for at least a short while, the torment he obviously still carried with him from that heartbreaking event.

She leaned forward, wrapped her arms around his neck and kissed him. Poured into that kiss the anguish she felt for him, the caring and compassion for all he'd endured, and yes, the deep attraction she'd felt from the first night they'd met.

CHAPTER TEN

THE SECOND HER mouth met his, she realized how much she'd missed kissing him. How foolish she'd been to resist this kind of intimacy with him, only letting herself now because she'd wanted, in some small way, to comfort him.

Except, for a long moment, Zeke didn't move as she held him in her arms. Didn't respond. Not pulling away, but not participating, either. She wondered if she'd been wrong to kiss him when he'd just shared such a tragedy with her, and a sliver of regret stabbed her heart. She began to ease back, a wisp of air now between their lips. Until she heard him groan just before his arms wrapped around her, smashed her body close to his, and he kissed her back.

But not with the kind of kiss he'd given

her before. It wasn't the sweet, delicious kiss they'd shared beneath the southern lights. This was intense and unrestrained and felt a little desperate. As though the emotions wrung out of him through sharing the pain of his past were being channeled into the way his mouth moved on hers. Into a passion and desire that would make him forget. Make them both forget, all thoughts gone except for the undeniable chemistry that had crackled between them from the beginning.

His mouth stayed on hers, and stayed, and it felt like they were nearly fused together, her head light, her body hot. Long minutes passed until, through the sensual fog in her mind, she realized the kiss had slowly changed. Had moved from how it had started, a little wild and untamed, to a different kind of emotion. Something more tender. Something deeper. Something intangible that shook her heart in a way that felt both a little scary and special beyond belief.

"Jordan." His voice unsteady, his mouth left hers to slide down her throat, to the pulse wildly beating there. "I want you. I've wanted you from that first minute we met in your cabin. Do you have any idea how hard it was to stop myself kissing you that night?"

"I might. Because I felt that way, too."

His mouth moved to her ear, nibbling and licking his way back to her mouth for another kiss so heavenly it made her quiver. She felt her heart give an odd little skip, and realized it was from relief as well as pleasure. That she'd been able to help him move past the painful emotions he'd shared, that they could smile together again, felt like the most gratifying thing she'd ever done.

His mouth moved on hers, their tongues tangling as the kiss breathlessly deepened, and for the briefest moment, a question flitted through her brain. Why in the world had she been so hesitant to give in to this *thing* they shared, and the way he made her feel? At that moment, it absolutely felt meant to be that they'd make love together. That it had been inevitable all along.

With that thought, she decided it should be her who made the first to move in that direction. Unwrapping her arms from around his neck, she reached for the buttons on his shirt. She fumbled with them, distracted by all the heady kissing, and finally got it open, shoving it off his shoulders. He assisted with pulling his arms from the sleeves, and she took advantage of that to slide her fingers beneath the T-shirt he wore under it. To feel his warm skin and the rough hair on his stomach and the way his flesh quivered at her touch made her quiver uncontrollably, too.

The minute the flannel shirt was off, he stripped the next layer from his body, exposing dark skin and rippling muscles. Slowly, she ran her hands over everything she could reach, in near awe at his physical beauty.

"I guess all that diving and heavy equipment is a good workout," she managed. "Unless it's working with plankton in the aquarium that makes you so sexy."

"It's the plankton. Nothing sexier than plankton." He reached for the sweatshirt she wore and pulled it over her head, his eyes glinting as they roamed her torso, his fingertip reaching to slowly stroke across the lace along the top of her bra. "Tell me what makes *you* so sexy, Dr. Flynn."

"That I can laparoscopically remove a gallbladder with the precision of a diamond cutter?"

"Ah. I love it when a woman talks dirty to me."

That familiar teasing grin was back on his face, and she grinned back, only to gasp a second later when he leaned in to place his mouth over her breast, gently sucking on her nipple through her bra. The sensation was so wildly erotic she could hardly breathe, and she held his head against her and moaned.

With her brain capable of no thought other than the incredible way he was making her feel, she considered it a very good thing that he took the initiative to move the two of them around on the small bed. One second she was sitting up, and the next she was lying on her back, staring up into his handsome face before he kissed her. Warm hands roamed over her, slipping off her bra, removing her jeans and underwear, then his own. Then he sat up, looking down at her with a heated gleam in his eyes as he stroked his long fingers slowly across her bare skin, making her gasp and wriggle at how amazingly good that simple touch felt.

Late sunlight streamed through the window, skimming across every muscle on his gloriously naked body and highlighting the proof that he was every bit as aroused as she felt, and her heart stuttered at the image before her.

Wow. If anyone ever asked her if Ezekiel Edwards was a remarkable specimen of manhood, she'd tell them *that* would be a complete understatement.

"I never realized it until this minute, but... I'm very thankful for plankton."

He laughed, then leaned down to kiss her again, his mouth sliding across her cheek to nuzzle her neck, then slowly on down to her breast, teasing one at a time. She gasped, then gasped again when his fingers found her core, touching and caressing until she could hardly bear it. Little mewling sounds came from her mouth, but she didn't even care—all she wanted was more of the way he made her feel.

Her own fingers explored his body, loving touching him as he brought her such unbearable pleasure. His hard, defined muscles, his smooth shoulders, his tight buttocks. She reached to clasp him in her hand, and loved that she made him shudder and groan. Part of her wanted this moment to go on forever, but she wanted him inside her even more.

She wrapped her legs around his hips and he took that as the invitation she'd intended, briefly pausing to take a condom from the bedside drawer and roll it on. When they joined together, they began moving in a rhythm so perfect it was like nothing she'd ever experienced before. Like feeling fused together on that dance floor, but even more incredible. His dark eyes looked into hers with such intensity, such deep desire, and his name left her lips on a heavy sigh.

"Zeke."

"Jordan," he whispered back, his hands moving to cup her face before his mouth joined hers once more. He gave, and she gave, both of them taking the pleasure each offered the other in a connection that felt so deep it was nearly unbearable. When they finally shattered, her heart filled with something that felt so big, so special, so unnerving, she feared it might never go quite back to normal again.

Zeke's eyes flew open and he abruptly sat up, his heart racing and sweat pouring down his back. He sucked in deep breaths to get himself under control.

The nightmare had been more vivid than usual, and he fought down the panic attack, running his hands up and down his face and rocking back and forth. A small sound had him sitting dead still, and he dropped his hands and opened his eyes.

Jordan. Jordan was asleep, right next to him. Right there.

Memories of the night before seemed to calm the horrible, shaky feeling. Tamped down the panic. His breathing slowed, and got easier. His heart quietly settled into a normal rhythm.

Her long eyelashes fanned her cheeks as she slept, and Zeke looked down at her beautiful face, a peculiar mix of emotions in his chest. From the moment he'd met her, a part of him had wished for this to happen between them, even knowing it shouldn't. For them to get to know one another, spend time together.

Now that wish had come true, and he wasn't sure it was the best thing for Jordan. Thinking of what they'd shared last night, of their time diving together and working together, even just watching her sleep, brought a smile to his lips that started deep inside him, near the region of his heart. At the same time, a sharp stab to that same general area reminded him that he had nothing to offer her. That he could never give her that home and roots and happy-ever-after she wanted. Was it wrong for him to want to be with her, knowing all he lacked inside?

He didn't know. All he knew was that he didn't want to walk away. Not yet. She knew about his past. And since she did, that meant she also understood his limitations, right?

He heaved a sigh and shook off his worries, for now. Her eyelids flickered and opened. When she looked up at him, the smile that started in their blue depths before forming on her lips had him forgetting about anything but how beautiful she was. About how incredibly lucky he was that she'd decided to be with him. For now.

"Good morning," she said, reaching up to stroke her finger down his cheek.

"Good morning. I'm glad you seemed to sleep just fine without your eye mask and noise machine."

"I must have felt exceptionally tired and relaxed, for some reason."

"Me, too. For some reason."

He'd become such a sucker for the laughter in her eyes, and leaned over to kiss her again, wishing they had time to lie in bed together for longer. Much longer. To make love for hours. But that would have to wait.

Reluctantly, he dragged his mouth from hers. "Want to come diving with me this morning? I need to get a few more samples to add to my data before I send in the grant application. And you need more data for your parents' ear device. Otherwise—" he tugged at the sheet covering her delectable body and ran his fingers across her skin, loving the way she wriggled and laughed "—I'd beg you to stay here as long as possible."

"When are you going?"

"I booked the van for eight-fifteen, and a couple of the new marine biologists and a tender are coming with me." Since it was after seven now, that was way, way too soon. If he'd known they'd be lying in bed together this morning, he'd never have scheduled it so early. "I already asked them if they'd like to participate in your trial, and everyone was interested."

"I appreciate that so much. And diving

sounds wonderful. But I'm afraid I can't go with you." Her lips puckered into a faux pout. "Dr. Bradshaw and the new nurse are traveling on the plane this morning to one of the other stations while the weather is good. He wants to evaluate how our new hospital and clinic compares to theirs, and see if we're ahead of the curve, or missing something."

Well, hell. Until she'd said she couldn't go, he hadn't even realized how much he wanted to dive with her again. Share her delight and see her amazement at all the Antarctic seas offered divers that they couldn't see anywhere else. "Will you look for a time in your schedule to go soon, and let me know when? Once I get the grant application finished and sent, I'll be diving most every day."

"I will. Believe me, I want to explore that incredible world again. With you."

The way she was looking at him made his heart beat harder, and he kissed her again, even as he knew he had to get going. Reluctantly, he broke the kiss and drew back. "It's a date. And when I wear the earplugs, you can check my vitals again. Though if you'd recorded them last night, my pulse and respiration would have been off-the-charts elevated."

"Mine, too." Her soft laughter sneaked into his chest and made him smile. "And that, Dr. Edwards, is a date I can't wait too long for."

That they couldn't share more than one quick kiss frustrated him beyond belief. But the crew would be waiting for him, and he had to go with them to collect the last samples he needed to finish the grant application. He pulled out clothes that would be warm enough for the excursion, letting himself watch Jordan as she got dressed. He admired her slim, athletic physique and her beautiful, smooth skin. Her round bottom and long legs.

Damn. It took all his willpower to keep from stripping off the clothes he'd just put on, to reach for her and kiss her and make love with her again, and to hell with the research.

He fought with his body's instantaneous reaction and tried to focus. "Want to grab a quick breakfast, before we both go to work?"

"Do you think people will wonder if we spent the night together?"

"I have no idea." It hadn't occurred to him that she'd worry about that, but he could see how someone wanting the husband and kids and picket fence might not want anyone to know about a short affair. "Would that bother you?"

Her eyes met his, a slight frown between her brows. Then the frown cleared, and she wrapped her arms around his neck, looking up at him with a clear gaze and look of trust that was gratifying at the same time it sent that stab of worry into his chest all over again. "No. It wouldn't bother me. No more questioning if it's a good idea or not. I want to be with you while we're here together."

He couldn't think of a thing to say in return, and even if he had, the tightness in his throat at what she'd said might have made it hard to talk. So he kissed her instead, telling her without words how much it meant to him that she wanted to be with him as much as he wanted to be with her. That she understood the limitations of what he could offer.

He looked into her eyes and swallowed hard. "Ready to grab that breakfast?" he asked, his voice gruff from their kiss and the conversation.

"Ready."

The galley wasn't crowded yet, and they sat with the men he would be diving with. Jordan talked with them about the earplugs and gave a pack to each of them. The person who would be their tender on this trip, a guy named Lance, showed up to tell them the van was packed and ready to go, and they all stood.

"See you around, Dr. Flynn," he said, trying to keep his voice normal and professional.

"Hope your dive goes well, Dr. Edwards." Her eyes met his, briefly transmitting the warmth and intimate feelings he'd been trying to keep to himself, before she turned to walk toward the hallway leading to the hospital.

He watched her go, and blew out a breath. Was he making a mistake here, and would she get hurt because of it?

The men traveling with him began asking questions about the distance to the dive hole and what he'd collected so far as they stowed the last of their personal gear. They all piled into the van, Zeke sitting in front next to Lance, who was behind the wheel. The men in back began comparing notes about some other research project they'd done together, and Zeke found his mind drifting to Jordan.

She'd loved her first trip driving through this vast, icy landscape when they'd gone to the dive hole together, and her delight had made him feel like he was seeing it with new eyes, too. He thought about diving with her, and how special that had been. Thought about the night they'd just shared, and how it had been way beyond special.

That he couldn't get her out of his head, hadn't been able to for days, made him face an uncomfortable truth. He was falling hard for her, and it would not be good for her to fall the same way, considering everything. What the hell he could do to make sure that didn't happen, he had no clue.

A strange, moaning sound came from Lance, and the oddness of it shook Zeke out of his worrisome thoughts. He looked over to see Lance was holding his stomach, a deep grimace etched on his face.

"What's wrong?"

"I…don't know. My stomach hurt a little this morning, and I didn't feel like eating. But now it's a real sharp pain."

"Where is the pain?"

"Right…here." He held his hand over the lower right side of his abdomen, and grunted again. "Man. It was just kind of a dull ache in the middle of my stomach this morning, but it's a whole lot worse, and lower, now."

Zeke frowned. The symptoms he described didn't really tell him much, and he turned to the men in the backseat. "Can one of you grab my medical bag from behind you? It's tucked into the side slot of the van."

One of them leaned over the seat to look around, coming up with the bag. "This it?"

"Yes. Thanks." Zeke unzipped the bag, looking for his thermometer. "Stop the van for a minute, Lance. I want to check your temperature. If—"

Zeke and the other two were thrown forward as Lance jammed on the brakes, barely stopping the vehicle before he flung open his door. He leaned over, vomiting onto the ice, which was a new symptom Zeke needed to consider. Maybe it was a simple virus, but appendicitis was another possibility. Even if that was unlikely, Lance needed to be seen and have some tests run right away.

"Damn, I'm so sorry." Lance sat back up

and wiped his mouth on his sleeve before looking over at Zeke, clutching at his stomach again.

"All right. No point in taking your temp now, or in trying to get this trip in, when you're feeling like this. We need to get you to the hospital so Dr. Flynn can check you out and see what's wrong."

"Hospital?" Lance looked shocked. "No, I probably have a bug or something. Don't you think?"

"Maybe. But your symptoms also could be from appendicitis, and waiting around to do something about that could result in a rupture. Believe me, you don't want that to happen." He'd seen it more than once, resulting in peritonitis, which was a serious infection. "We're switching seats, and going back to the station."

Once he was behind the wheel, he turned to talk to the men in back. "I won't be able to go with you today, but I think there's a good chance you can find a few others to join you. It's early enough that you can still get a mostly full day under the ice, if you do."

They nodded and looked at Lance, obviously understanding why they had to go back, which Zeke was glad about. There had been times when scientists he knew got so focused on the work they had to get done that, when something went wrong, they got frustrated and argued about the right course of action.

Things happened sometimes that couldn't be controlled. And that something was happening today. Which meant he would be one more day behind where he'd wanted to be to get his grant work finished and submitted.

He held in a deep sigh and hit the gas, wanting to get Lance to Jordan as soon as possible. He'd just have to work harder and smarter in less time. And he hoped that wouldn't mean he couldn't spend much time with Jordan until it was done.

CHAPTER ELEVEN

BEING IN THE hospital so early meant Jordan could get the paperwork finished that she'd set aside while working on the newest round of baseline physicals. With Tony and Megan gone for the day, she'd decided not to schedule too many appointments in a row, in case there was an emergency she had to deal with.

Which had proven to be a good decision, though she hadn't known at the time that it would have nothing to do with taking care of an emergency patient. Functioning even after drinking several cups of coffee was proving to be a little difficult, since she felt pretty exhausted after the night she'd spent with Zeke. Exhausted, but exhilarated.

If she'd known what a fantastic lover the man would be, she wouldn't have held him at arm's length, though even as the thought came, that niggle of worry she'd had from the beginning poked again. Ezekiel Edwards was head and shoulders above any man she'd been involved with before, both literally and figuratively. Would it be hard to fall in love with someone back in England, having known Zeke?

No. It would be okay. She loved adventuring beneath the water with him and out in the field here, but she also knew very well that he wasn't the man she'd spend her life with. So she was going to let herself enjoy being with him for the "now" and remember him fondly when it was over.

If only she could have gone diving with him today. Hopefully, there would be plenty of other days when they'd be under the ice together. Months of fun with him, exploring with him, making love with him.

Elation filled her chest and she tapped away at the computer with renewed energy. Living in Antarctica was going to be a whole lot more interesting than she'd ever dreamed it might be, in a way she hadn't imagined.

The clack of the hospital's swinging doors had her turning in surprise to see who might be coming in. Then was even more surprised when she saw Zeke. A man was with him, walking a little hunched over, his face pinched and drawn.

She hurried over. "Tell me what's wrong."

"Stomach hurts. A lot. Right here." The man pointed at his lower right abdomen.

"Lance was driving us to the site, planning to work as our tender," Zeke said. "Experiencing belly pain and vomiting. I haven't taken his temperature, but I knew there was a slight risk of it being appendicitis, and didn't want to wait for him to see you."

She looked up at Zeke, impressed yet again at his medical skills to even think of that. The symptoms were so vague most people would just assume he was sick with a virus. "All right. Lance, we'll start with a urine test, then I want to do an ultrasound and take a look at your appendix. Will you help him to the bathroom, Zeke? The sample bottles are in the cabinet above the sink. When you're done, I want you to take off your shirt and pants and put on a paper gown, open in the front. You can leave on your underwear."

"Okay."

"This way, Lance," Zeke said.

Her eyes met Zeke's as he gave her a quick nod and one of his trademark knee-weakening smiles. She got the ultrasound machine and gel ready, and when they returned, Zeke handed her the sample bottle.

"For you."

Something about the way he said it made her want to laugh. "Thank you. You're a peach."

"So, why did you want the urine sample?" Lance asked, pressing his hand to his stomach again as he nearly doubled over.

"To see if you might have a urinary tract infection." She held up the bottle and it looked clear, not cloudy, but she'd check it with a dipstick after the ultrasound, if that test wasn't conclusive. "I'm sorry you're in pain, but we're going to figure this out as quickly as we can. Please lie down on the exam table."

She rolled some ultrasound gel around Lance's belly, following with the wand. She studied the picture on the monitor as she slowly moved the wand across his skin, and saw that Zeke was staring at the images, as well, his brows lowered in concentration.

Sometimes ultrasound was inconclusive. But today, they were lucky. Zeke's eyes met hers, and she gave him a wide smile and nodding salute, because he deserved it.

"Dr. Edwards might not be a medical doctor, but he knows his stuff, Lance. You do have appendicitis, and figuring that out is the first big step. Next step? You're going to need an appendectomy."

"Ah, hell. You mean surgery?"

"I'm afraid so. We have to remove your appendix before it has a chance to rupture. But I'll do it laparoscopically, which means small incisions and less recovery time than traditional surgery."

"Dr. Flynn informed me earlier that she has the skilled precision of a diamond cutter when using a laparoscope. So you're in luck, Lance."

The amusement, and something else, in his eyes as they met hers had her nearly choking trying not to laugh, which wouldn't be very professional. Neither would letting her mind go to what they'd been doing when she'd said that...

She turned to the patient, getting her head back to her job. "I have done a lot of these procedures, so you don't need to worry. I'm going to give you antibiotics beforehand, then a general anesthetic to put you to sleep, so you won't feel a thing."

"How long will I have to be off work?"

"After a couple days of rest you'll be able to do light work. But no heavy lifting until you've had at least two weeks to heal." She looked up at Zeke, so glad that, with Megan gone, he was there with her. Doing this procedure alone would have been a lot more difficult, though she felt bad she had to lean on him yet again.

"I'm sorry to ask, but can you assist? I know you need to get diving, but having you here would be a huge help. Not very good timing for both Megan and Tony to be gone."

"I've never assisted with a surgery before, but I think I can figure it out."

"I know you can." She knew Zeke Edwards was smart and capable of pretty much anything he set his mind to. And it bothered her that, after what happened to his grandparents, he didn't seem to believe that about himself.

She gave Lance the antibiotic, administered the anesthesia, then got to work. Zeke proved to be an excellent assistant, not that she was surprised. With him responding to her every request, it all went smoothly, and when the surgery was over, she snapped off her gloves and lowered her mask to give him a big smile of thanks.

"You were awesome. Are you sure you don't want to add medical doctor to your list of advanced degrees?"

"I think two are enough." He returned her smile. "And I can confirm that 'diamond cutter' is a good way to describe your surgical skills, Dr. Flynn. Congratulations."

"Thanks. We make a good team."

"We do."

Their eyes met again. That crazy connection between them seemed to vibrate in the room, and the way he was looking at her, a little like she imagined a hungry leopard seal might look, made her feel breathless.

"Are you okay here alone now?" he asked. "I'll stay if you really need me, but I'd like to get to the dive site as soon as I can. I'm already behind on getting everything I need for the grant, so showing up late today is better than not at all."

"Go dive. With the surgery finished, I'm fine here alone." Somehow, despite the conversation being about work, her heart did that fluttering thing again, times ten. Because now she knew how beautiful he was beneath those clothes, how it felt to lie with him skin to skin, how it felt to make love with him.

He must have seen it in her eyes, since he closed the gap between them, drew her close and kissed her. When they separated, the seriousness of his expression seemed at odds with his light words.

"Hold that thought, Dr. Flynn. Until tonight."

She lifted shaking fingertips to her lips as she watched him leave. She'd thought living in Antarctica meant nonstop cold? How wrong she'd been. Being around Zeke Edwards definitely made her feel very, very hot. And she had a feeling it would seem like a very long day until she got to be with him again.

Feeling a little like a giddy teenager was not the way to get her work done, and Jordan checked on Lance, pleased to see he was doing well after waking from the anesthesia.

She gave him pain medication, then doubled down on the paperwork she had to finish. A couple of people came into the clinic to bring medical supplies that had arrived with the latest boat, and she absently pointed them to the supply closet.

Then did a double take. She stood to stare before they went into the room to stash the items they'd brought.

Was that...was that Weston MacIntyre? Lia's ex-boyfriend? Ex-fiancé? The guy who'd practically left her at the altar? The man who had completely disappeared from sight, not letting Lia or anyone else know where he'd gone?

Her heart beating double time, she crept to peek into the supply room. Sure enough, it was West who was taking boxes from the wheeled cart and stacking them on shelves.

Oh, my Lord. She practically ran back to hide behind the computer while her mind raced. Should she go talk to him? Let him know she'd seen him? Or should she let Lia know first?

Lia. Lia was her best friend, and after looking for West for who knew how long she deserved to know.

Jordan grabbed the satellite phone, having no idea if it would be working or not, and felt a little limp with relief when she got a dial tone. She shakily punched in Lia's number, and waited.

"Ophelia Monterrosa."

"Lia," she whispered, glancing up to make sure West wasn't coming her way. "It's Jordan. Are you sitting down?"

"What? Is something wrong?"

"I'm working in the hospital and clinic alone today. And who walks in but…are you ready? Weston MacIntyre."

"What?" Lia's voice rose to a squeak. "Are you kidding me? He's in Antarctica?"

"He's in Antarctica. Alive and well."

"Antarctica. *Antarctica.* No wonder I couldn't find him! The rat bastard!"

"I know a group just came here from another station last night. Since I haven't seen him in the galley or anywhere else, maybe he was there for the winter, then working in this new station for the summer. Or maybe not. Obviously, I have no idea what he's been up to. Want me to talk to him? Ask him anything?"

Lia was silent at the other end for a long

moment before she answered. "No. No, I'm coming down there."

Jordan lifted the phone from her ear and stared. She was going to make the trek all the way to the south pole to confront the man who'd broken her heart?

"Are you sure? I thought you were dealing with difficult things at home."

"I am, but it can wait a short time. I'd actually been thinking about that job opportunity you told me about. So I'm finding a way to get down there and do some work. I need to see him face-to-face. I've been looking for him for months, and I'm not waiting more months to make that happen, now that I know where he is."

"Wow, you amaze me. Always have, of course! Let me know when you might get here, okay?"

"I will. And please don't let him know you've seen him, if at all possible. I want it to be a surprise."

Her friend's hard voice was totally different from anything Jordan had heard come out of her mouth before, and she almost felt sorry for West, having to deal with a furious, betrayed Lia. Almost. But the man had hurt her badly, and deserved whatever Lia planned to throw at him.

"I'll steer clear from him if I can. And, Lia?"

"Yes?"

"Best of luck and safe travels. I can't believe I'm going to get to see you here in Antarctica, but I can't wait."

Held close in the warmth of Zeke's arms as they lay in his bed together had Jordan wishing that they could stay here together all morning and forget work and the outside world. Just as she had yesterday, and the day before that, and for every one of the seven glorious nights and mornings they'd spent together. The only thing making her feel better about leaving the pleasure of their naked bodies pressed to one another was her excitement about getting to dive with him.

"What time did you say you reserved the van to go out to the dive hole?" she asked.

"Not until after two." His warm palm stroked her hair as he looked down at her. "But now that we have twenty-four-hour daylight down here, getting started late doesn't matter so much. I have work I've got to finish in the aquarium this morning, but we'll still be able to get in a decent day's dive."

Her pleasure-fogged brain finally registered that his usual relaxed or teasing expression wasn't there this morning, and she looked at him a little more carefully. There was a slight tenseness etched there, some distance, even, like his mind wasn't as focused on their naked bodies pressed together as hers was.

Her heart gave a little lurch, wondering what he might be thinking about, and if he was concerned about the two of them spending every night laughing and talking and making love. If maybe he felt uneasy about so much togetherness. That she might be starting to expect more than he wanted to give, since they both knew this couldn't be anything more than a short-term fling. Then the second the thought came, she wanted to thrash herself.

Was she becoming the kind of woman who got all needy and clingy? Wanting constant reassurance that things were still good between them?

No. Absolutely not. She might have a serious crush on the man, and have a hard time not thinking about him whenever she had a spare minute. But that was it. She'd gone into this knowing exactly what they could, and couldn't, have together. "You have a lot to do still, before your grant application is ready to go?"

"Yeah. Too much. Mostly the last of the lab work, then compiling the data. I got behind. But I'll get it done."

His chest lifted in a deep sigh, and she rested her palm on his warm sternum, gently stroking his chest, hoping to ease the anxiety he was clearly feeling, and that she was suddenly feeling now, too. "If…spending time with me is why you're behind and feeling stressed about it, I'm sorry. And I'll stay out of the way until you're finished."

"Not why I'm behind. Or, at least, not the only reason. I admit that I would have gotten more work done if I hadn't had beautiful you as a distraction." He grasped her hand and held it to his chest, and she felt relieved that his lips had curved into a small smile. "But being with you is also a stress reliever. I'll be okay."

"About today, though. If you're going diving just for me, we don't have to. I'd rather you get your work done." Not going to the dive site would be disappointing, since she had the whole day off. But his not feeling stressed about finishing the research? A whole lot more important than her figuring out what to do with herself.

"I think it'll be okay." He dropped a kiss to her forehead, slid his warm lips to her temple. "Besides, we haven't been able to go diving together since that first time. We're way overdue. I want to share that underwater world with you again."

"Okay. But only if you're sure."

"I'm sure."

As if to prove that, he wrapped his arms around her and kissed her. Probably he'd intended it to be a short and sweet touch of their lips before they got up to get on with the day. For him to get to the aquarium as soon as possible. But as always seemed to happen between them, the kiss turned hotter, deeper. He rolled her onto his chest, his fingers tunneling in her hair, then moving to curl around her nape as he held her mouth against his. They both gasped, the kiss becoming frenzied, and she opened her eyes to see his lids lifting, too. His eyes nearly black, they shone with a desire that reflected exactly how she felt.

God, she wanted to somehow be even closer, and after helping him put on a condom she rose to straddle him. To take him in. They moved together, and the pleasure was nearly unbearable, and she wanted to feel all of him, his soft skin and hard muscle and rough hair, against her. Her hair spilled across his chest as she leaned forward, breast to chest, a deep groan exploding from his chest as he grasped her hips.

"Jordan. You're killing me here."

"Not ready for you to go. Not yet."

A rough laugh left his lips and she chuckled softly at the joke, too, before their mouths joined again. Except this kiss seemed to make her heart squeeze hard in her chest, and when they both climaxed, the truth struck her like a blow.

Not yet? Not ready for him to go?

The truth was, maybe she never would be. And that felt scary as hell.

CHAPTER TWELVE

ZEKE STOOD AT the lab tables set up next to
the aquarium and worked on measuring and
tagging the crabs he'd collected during his
last dive, ticked at himself all over again.

Lying next to Jordan's delicious body, he
hadn't wanted to move from that bed, even
as he'd been thinking about how behind he
was, and how he'd have to double his efforts to get the last of the research done and
the data recorded and the paper finished on
time. He'd told her he'd go on the dive with
her, even though he damn well just didn't
have time today.

Then he'd kissed her. Had meant for it
to be a goodbye-for-now kiss, so he could
get up and tackle the work he had to catch
up on. But what happened? The second his
mouth met hers, he was a goner. All worries

from just a moment earlier vanished from his brain, and the only thing that seemed to matter was her. How good it felt to kiss her and touch her, and how he wanted more of all that. And when she rose above him, her eyes shining as she looked down, her soft hair skimming across his skin as she bent forward to kiss him again, his heart seemed to stutter, then nearly stop.

Somehow, in the span of just a few weeks, Jordan had taken possession of his heart and soul in a way he'd never experienced before. And for several reasons, he knew this was serious cause for concern.

He put the crab into the aquarium box he'd be taking back to the water and snapped off his gloves. He ran his hands down his face and drew a deep breath before picking up a pencil to make some research notes, and for the first time in his life, his attention was only half on his work.

Having to face that he'd fallen hard for Jordan wasn't really the problem. The loss of his grandparents had taught him he could live through the most difficult times life could throw at him. When he and Jordan parted ways, he knew it would hurt like hell, something new for him when it came to the end of an ice affair. But he could handle it.

The problem was her, and any future sadness that would be his fault. The closeness they shared was real and intense, and he knew she felt that intangible connection every bit as acutely as he did. No matter how much she claimed to understand his limitations, and that what the two of them were experiencing now didn't fit into her future plans, he had a bad feeling it might hurt her, anyway.

He reached into the aquarium for another crab, his mind still only half on what he was doing, the other half on Jordan. He knew if he told her he felt worried about her being hurt, she'd tell him he was being an egotistical idiot and that she'd be fine. Maybe she would be. But how could he be sure?

He couldn't. And maybe that was just life. A part of life he had to accept. She wasn't trusting him to be there for her in a way he couldn't be, and he'd never put her in a position where he'd fail her that way.

The thought lifted his spirits a little, even as he shook his head at himself. Bottom line was, he didn't want their relationship to end until the expedition was over. Wanted to be with her as much as possible until then, and he was doing a damn good job convincing himself it would all be okay.

"How's it going in here?"

He turned at the sound of Jordan's upbeat voice, and just seeing her made him smile, despite all his confusion of just a moment ago.

"Making progress, but still way behind."

She came to stand next to him, peering into the aquarium. "This is so cool. Sometime, will you tell me more about the research you're doing? I'd love to know more about it."

"As soon as I have this grant-application monkey off my back, I'd be happy to."

"Thanks. So. Here's the plan for today." She planted her hands on his shoulders, surprising him with a steely look of determination. "I've been thinking. There's no reason for you to dive with me today, when you have all this work to do here. I'll just go with the other divers, so I can be there when they test the earbuds. Now that I've been under the water once, I have a better idea what it's like. You and I will dive another time. We've got months left here together, right?"

He looked into the serious deep blue of her eyes, struggling with what to do. He wanted to go with her. Wanted to spend time with her beneath the ice again. Also wanted make sure she was safe, even though that was probably absurd. She knew how to dive, and would be with other experienced divers. There wasn't anything he could do for her that they couldn't do, too, if something went wrong.

And he did have a hell of a lot of work left, and only a few days to finish it. He might have had trouble making it his number one priority with Jordan around, but the truth was, he had to make that happen for the rest of this week to make sure he got the application in on time.

"I really want to go." He put his hands on her hips and tugged her close. "But you're right. I should stay here and finish. After it's done, we'll dive. And do other things."

"Other things?" Her hands slid up around his neck and her face relaxed into the confident, amused, adorable Jordan he'd fallen for that very first night in her cabin.

"Things like finding sea butterflies and jellyfish. Things like finding the penguin rookeries. And...things."

A soft laugh left her lips before they touched his, warm and soft and sweet, and he was grateful she was the first to pull away because he wouldn't have been able to. Instead, he had a feeling he might have danced them over to the photography dark room, stripped them both naked and made love with her again, making her miss her dive and him late with his work, for certain.

"I look forward to all of those...things, Dr. Edwards." One more kiss, then she stepped back, the twinkle fading from her eyes. "Tonight, I think I'll hang out with a few of the people I've met the past couple weeks, then go to my own cabin. So you can get your work done."

He opened his mouth to protest, then closed it, glad one of them was thinking clearly. And maybe that meant he'd been wrong to be worried about her getting hurt and missing him when it was over.

Maybe the truth was, when that time came, he'd be the only one dealing with a seriously bruised heart.

* * *

As they drove along the marked road, Jordan talked with Bob and the two scientists who would be diving that day. Ronald Reardon and Maggie Schindler, both marine biologists, enjoyed talking about their work and their trips to Antarctica, and Jordan enjoyed listening, even as she wished Zeke was there to share some of his stories, too.

The van finally arrived at the dive site, and the sunlight on the ice and snow was nearly blinding. Jordan couldn't wait to get into the water to see how much the light would be filtering through. When she'd dived with Zeke that first time, it had been a fairly gray day, and still, the surprising brightness of the water, illuminating the seafloor and all its inhabitants, had amazed her.

As she pulled her gear from the van, she realized she'd been thinking of him that entire day. That it felt weirdly wrong to be here without him, as though, somehow, he and she and diving in that frigid ocean were unforgettably intertwined. But he needed to get his work done. When he did, the stress she'd noticed on his face this week would hopefully be gone, and they'd be able to enjoy more special times again that she knew she'd carry with her forever.

Her heart pinched, and the deep, cold breath she drew into her lungs made her chest hurt. Saying goodbye to him when the time came was not going to be easy.

Maybe he won't want to say goodbye.

The thought came without permission, and she fiercely battled it back. She'd gone into this thing with him knowing he never wanted any kind of committed relationship, and she wanted a completely different kind of life than the kind a traveling scientist could offer her. Stupid thoughts of a future were just that: stupid. And she wasn't stupid.

Determined to put those thoughts away for good, she hauled all her dive gear from the van and lugged them to the dive hole. It wasn't the same one she'd gone through with Zeke. This one was bigger, and didn't have a tent over it since the weather was getting warmer and the winds were generally calmer, though Zeke had told her that could change in an instant down here.

The four of them stood at the edge of the hole and finished getting ready. "Let me tie the rope onto your belt, Jordan," Bob said.

"Thanks. It feels so different to be out here in the open, instead of inside that little tent, like before. And this hole is huge! I thought Zeke said they'd cut the two the same size."

"He brought the crew out here with the chain saws to make it bigger a few days ago. Said it gets too crowded when more people are diving at the same time, and it's easy to make it big when you don't need a tent."

"That makes sense." She wriggled into the dry suit, and she couldn't seem to help that the memories came again. She and Zeke alone in the dive tent. Zeke helping her tug the suit up her body...

"Jordan, can you hand me my goggles? Sorry, but I dropped them on top of yours," Maggie said.

"Uh, sure." If she couldn't keep her mind on what needed to happen to get ready, she shouldn't even have come. "Here are the earplugs, too. And yours, Ronald. I really appreciate you both trying them."

"Interesting concept I'm happy to try," he said. He tucked them into his ears before pulling everything else over his head, then sat at the edge of the hole. "Here I go. Last one in is a rotten egg."

Maggie laughed and shook her head. "You always—*aahh!*"

Her shriek came just seconds before Ronald, Jordan and Bob screamed, too, as a leopard seal nearly as long as the van surged out of the water, rested its wide chest on the ice shelf and clamped its teeth on Ronald's leg, violently shaking him like a rag doll. The momentum sent Ronald's shoulders swinging into Jordan's legs and she fell with a crash onto the ice, knocking the wind from her lungs. With her heart pounding like a jackhammer in her throat, she tried to scramble backward like a crab, away from the monster, not getting enough traction on the slippery ice as terror gripped her. Staring into the creature's slit-like yellow eyes and sharklike teeth, she thought she might be looking at some giant prehistoric lizard come back to life in the Antarctic.

Bob acted first, grabbing one of the scuba tanks and slamming it onto the seal's back. Her breath coming in ragged gasps, Jordan took his lead and grabbed one, too, swinging it at the terrifying mouth that had such a grip on Ronald. The blow turned out to be little more than a glancing one, but combined with Bob's efforts, the seal let go, sliding halfway down into the water, its head still staring at them with what for all the world looked like a leering smile.

"My God." Bob stepped over Jordan as she rolled to her knees, and adrenaline poured through her veins as the three of them grabbed Ronald by the armpits and pulled the groaning man out of the water. No way were they safe with that creature so close and they kept going, dragging the poor man away to put some distance between them and the leopard seal still glaring at them, leaving a bloody trail across the ice.

"Leopard seals…" Maggie said, her voice a gasp. "They usually won't follow us this far out of the water. But to be safe we need to get to the van."

"And we need to hurry," Jordan managed to say, grimly noting the wide swath of red spreading on the snow. "He's bleeding badly. I need to get a tourniquet on the wounds, then get him back to the hospital as fast as possible so I can evaluate what has to happen."

She studied Ronald's face as the three of them awkwardly lifted him to carry him to the van, trying to determine if he was going into shock, expecting that he was. "Let's make room to lay him in the back, and elevate his feet. We'll worry about getting the equipment later."

"Agreed," Maggie said.

"I'll drive," Bob said as they got Ronald settled into the cargo space of the van as carefully as they could, with Jordan climbing in after him to work on his leg. "Maggie, you're in the backseat to help Jordan with whatever she needs."

"Hang in there, Ronald. You're going to be okay." Jordan said it with a confidence she didn't entirely feel. The gaping tears in his flesh weren't like anything she'd had to deal with before, but she called on all her surgical training to take care of him the best she could.

As though they'd done this before, the three of them worked in a strangely choreographed way, with Maggie helping to pull bandages and other supplies from the medical case in the van and Bob driving far faster than Jordan would have ever expected he'd be comfortable with on the icy road.

Jordan got a tourniquet on Ronald's thigh to slow the bleeding, and got to work applying pressure to the multiple gashes and wounds, with Maggie assisting. God, if only Zeke was there with her. Yes, she was a well-trained surgeon and doctor and knew her stuff, when it came to hospital medicine.

Saving someone from bleeding out, far from a medical facility? That was where Zeke was the expert.

She swallowed hard, and intently focused on trying to get the bleeding stopped. Zeke wasn't here, and it was up to her to save Ronald's life.

Elbow-deep in the aquarium as he worked to gather the samples he still needed for the database that would motivate those offering the grants for addition work, Zeke decided not to answer the in-station phone jangling on the lab desk ten feet away.

He barely glanced at it before turning back to his task. Probably an unimportant call to the aquarium lab or one of the scientists working there, and if it was more than that, they'd leave a message. Or come to the lab themselves to find whoever it was they were calling.

It wouldn't be Jordan, because she'd decided to spend time with new friends to give him work space, and he appreciated that she understood how important it was to get this done. If she needed him for something right away, she'd come to the lab herself, wouldn't she?

The phone rang again, and something about its insistence had him heaving a sigh and stripping off one of his gloves to pick it up.

"Ezekiel Edwards."

"Zeke. It's Maggie. We have an emergency."

"What emergency?" He straightened, alarm skittering through his veins. Maggie had gone on the dive this afternoon. The dive with Jordan.

"Ronald's been hurt. We've just now gotten back to Fletcher. Jordan and Bob are rushing him to the hospital, and I thought you might be able to help."

"What?" For a split second, he felt frozen

in place as her words penetrated his brain. One second later, he'd yanked his other glove from his hand and was heading toward the hospital in a near run. "What happened?"

"A leopard seal bit him. Bad. I've never seen anything like it."

"Where were you and Bob when it happened?" He tried to suck in air. "And Jordan?"

"Right next to him. One second Ronald was sitting on the ice shelf, about to dive, and the next, the seal had lunged out of the water to grab him. Knocked Jordan over, too, but she's okay. Bob and Jordan grabbed scuba tanks and slammed them down onto the seal, and it finally let Ron go. But he's lost a lot of blood. I'm…scared."

His heart hammered in his chest. Poor Ron. God, he hoped he'd be okay. And Jordan had been right there next to him? Knocked down by the deadliest creature in these oceans? Knowing it could easily have been her the seal grabbed and nearly killed made it hard to breathe.

He burst through the hospital doors and saw Bob and Maggie both sitting in chairs, looking pale and worried. "Maggie told me it's bad. I'm going in to see if Jordan could use a hand."

"That would be good. Megan is assisting her, but the tears in his leg…so many." He could see Bob working to sound calm. "It was unbelievable. Not sure I can ever tender for anyone again."

"What we do down here always carries risk. We just have to do what we can to reduce it."

Easy to say. To know and accept. But not when it came to someone who was diving for fun. Jordan probably never should have been there to begin with, since diving wasn't part of her work here, other than the trial, and other divers were participating in that, anyway. But when she did go? He hadn't gone with her, to make sure she stayed safe. Had opted to leave her on her own, and what did that make him?

The same man he'd always been. A man who hadn't been there when they'd needed him most.

The weight of that failure hung in his chest as he quickly scrubbed, then went into the small operating room. He stared at the blood spattering the floor, the gurney, the front of Jordan's gown and her gloved hands as she leaned in, stitching closed the ragged wounds on Ronald's leg. Megan stood by, assisting.

"Jordan." He could barely get her name out, and tried again. "I'm here to help." He recognized the irony of his words. Showing up to help when the worst was over didn't say much for him, did it?

"Zeke." She glanced up, and the relieved smile she sent him was one he knew he didn't deserve. "Why don't you work on the cuts at the back of his calf while I finish these on the front. It's been hard to control the bleeding, and the sooner the gashes are closed, the better."

Silently, they worked together until all the wounds were stitched and wrapped. Jordan checked Ronald's vitals and nodded. "Good. He's stable. I gave him antibiotics when he first came in, and we'll need to follow with another dose in a few hours. Here are the rest of the instructions, Megan, and I'll be back to check his vitals again in a little while, if you can keep an eye on him until then."

"Got it," Megan said.

Jordan moved to the small scrub room and he followed. Both of them took off their bloody gowns. The second hers was off she stepped to him, wrapping her arms around him and leaning her head against his chest. He held her close, and the adrenaline of getting the wounds closed as fast as possible seeped away, leaving him feeling shaken, both physically and emotionally.

"That was...so terrifying," Jordan said, her voice muffled in his chest. "I can't even describe it."

"What exactly happened?"

"Ron was sitting on the side of the dive hole, ready to go in, when the seal just burst from the water and grabbed him. For a horrifying second, I thought it was going to drag him underwater, but it just shook him, its teeth deep in his leg and ripping..."

He didn't know what to say. Leopard seals had hovered around threateningly before, and he'd always kept his distance. Never had he come close to one actually attacking him or someone else.

Iciness crept through his veins and he could barely breathe, picturing what Jordan described. Ron could have been dragged underwater. Or bitten on his torso. Or bled to death, and it was a damn good thing Jordan had been there to deal with his wounds, and probably saved his life.

Or it could have been her. Her leg and body. Her blood. Her nearly killed or actually killed.

Ronald had been lucky. She might not have been.

"Where were you?"

"Next to him. Getting ready to go in." She leaned back and looked up at him, a wobbly smile on her lips. "It's almost a blur, at the same time it's so vivid in my mind it's like watching a movie. Except I was in it."

He covered her hand with his, and that connection soothed, a tiny bit, the raw chaos burning in his chest at what happened, and what could have happened.

"I'm...sorry you went through this."

"I so wished you were there," she whispered. "When he was bleeding so badly and from so many wounds, I was really afraid I couldn't get it stopped. Knew that you being with me might make all the difference."

"But I wasn't there. Wasn't there for him.

Or you. And you handled it fine on your own."

"We got lucky, I think." Maybe it was something in his tone, because she tipped her head and looked at him with a question in her eyes. "Is something wrong?"

"Yes. I'm what's wrong." He lifted his hand to her face and stroked his thumb across her cheek. Tried to imprint her beautiful face in his memory forever, as the reality of what happened today slammed into him all over again.

"What do you mean?"

"I wasn't there for Ron today. Not there for you," he said again. Everything inside him seemed to squeeze until it was hard to breathe. His heart was pounding, he started to sweat, and he worked to shove down the panic attack that threatened to overwhelm him. "I told you I can't be counted on to be there for anyone. Ever. And I wasn't."

"Zeke." Her brow creased in a perplexed frown. "You can't be everywhere, all the time. Things happen. Bad things. You did your best for your grandparents, and have to believe that. You would have done your best for Ronald, and for me, too, if you'd been there today."

"But I wasn't." He knew it was a dogged refrain, but she needed to hear him, damn it. "This is why I can't be close to anyone. Let anyone close to me. I can't be who you want, and who you deserve. You know that. And I hope you find that person. I truly do."

"Zeke—"

"Goodbye, Jordan." He let himself kiss her forehead, one last time. Stared into the beautiful blue of her eyes, a storm of emotion in his chest at the confusion and pain he saw there. But leaving now was for her own good. "You're going to have an awesome life, I know it. Take care."

Somehow, he forced himself to turn and go. To walk out the door and not look back, even as he finally admitted to himself that he loved her in a way he'd never loved a woman before.

It was a struggle to put one foot in front of the other, as though his feet were filled with lead, and he wondered if she could hear his heart cracking as the door closed behind him.

CHAPTER THIRTEEN

JORDAN SAT ON the floor of the supply room and refilled items in the field bags, which made her think about Zeke. Then she scoffed at herself. Who was she kidding? She'd thought of him way too much in the three weeks since he'd said goodbye, and wondered how long it would take for her to get over him. She knew that was pathetic, and even stupid, because their affair had always had an expiration date.

She just hadn't expected it to come so soon.

Ezekiel Edwards was a wonderful man in so many ways, and she knew that. It was so clear that he still felt tortured over the way his grandparents had died, and carrying that heavy load still deeply affected who he was today. A man who protected himself from pain by keeping an emotional distance. Refused to let himself get too close to anyone, and yet he felt responsible for everyone. She knew that had to be a difficult way to live, but he'd entrenched himself in that belief so deeply, and for so long, she had a feeling he'd stay there for the rest of his life.

For at least a week after he'd told her goodbye, she'd wanted to find him and rant. To tell him he needed to deal with his past and his guilt so he could move on with his life.

Let himself love someone. Let her love him.

Tears threatened and she heaved in a shuddery sigh. It wasn't until he'd walked out the door of the hospital that she finally admitted it to herself. She had fallen in love with him. And that love had turned on its head every conviction she'd been so certain about.

She loved him, and loved diving with him and being with him, but that was only part of why she loved this adventure in Antarctica. She loved sliding across the brilliant, frozen landscape on the Ski-Doo. Loved camping in a tent in the icy wilderness.

Loved excursions to see the penguin rookeries and the wildlife. And all that love had made her see what her childhood longings had blinded her to.

A safe and steady life with a safe and steady husband and putting down roots in a safe and steady suburb surrounded by a white picket fence wasn't what she wanted at all. She'd loved the adventures she'd had as a kid with her parents. Exploring the world was a big part of who she was, and Zeke helped her see that's still who she was. How she wanted to live her life. How she wanted her future children to live their lives.

Problem was, Zeke didn't want to live it with her. He probably wouldn't admit it, but he was the one who wanted the safe and steady, at least when it came to his heart. He kept it inside a cage and refused to let it out and give it to her.

She thought about the stricken look on his face the last time she'd seen him. Thought about the pain he'd held in his heart for so long. Maybe she'd been wrong to not find him and rant, after all. Or at least try to talk to him, to tell him how being with him had helped her see what she really wanted for her life. Find out if he'd let her help him see his own life in a different way than he'd been allowing himself to see it.

Was that possible at all? Would he be willing to listen? Or was it just a foolish pipe dream?

"Jordan." Tony Bradshaw walked into the supply room and interrupted her deep thoughts. "We have an injured patient in the field. Sounds like something you can handle there, without bringing her back, but you'll have to determine that when you get there. If you're willing to go?"

"Of course." She stood, then her heart skipped as a thought came to mind. "Um, who would go with me?"

"I asked the crew member you did surgery on. Lance." The medical director smiled. "He's feeling good now, and since he's grateful to you for diagnosing him, he said he'd be happy to go."

It was actually Zeke who'd done the initial diagnosis, and her heart ached all over again, remembering how well they'd worked together. "Glad to hear that. Is he ready to go?"

"He's packing the snow machine now. Said to meet him in the hangar."

"I'll grab my field bags and my coat and stuff, then I'll be ready. I'll keep you posted."

"Thank you. See you when you get back."

She gathered the field bags and headed to the hangar as memories of Zeke and their field trip clogged her throat. Kissing beneath the aurora australis. Intimately sharing that tent.

That trip was when she'd first started to realize she was falling in love with him, and still she'd told him all about how she'd wanted a safe and steady husband and that picket fence life, because she hadn't admitted to herself quite yet how she felt about him.

His beautiful dark eyes swam in front of her and she decided that, good outcome or bad, she'd be talking with Ezekiel Edwards as soon as she got back to Fletcher Station.

Zeke sat at the table in his cabin, holding the letter in his hand that should have him jumping with joy and celebrating.

The grant he'd worked so hard for had

been officially offered to him. His goal of working to impact the negative consequences of climate change was ensured for another year. He waited for the feeling of joy to lift his chest, but it didn't come.

Of course, he knew why. Because he didn't have Jordan to celebrate with him.

The past weeks had been hell. Across the room in the galley, he'd often see her smiling face and shining hair and hear her laughter as she sat with new friends. Most of the time she ignored him, but on the rare occasions that their eyes met, she looked so serious, so sad, that he usually got up and left the room, hating that he was the reason she felt that way.

He'd never meant for it to happen. Somehow, though, he hadn't been able to keep his distance from her, never fully understanding why. He'd been powerless to resist the magnetic attraction he'd felt, even knowing she might get hurt.

Actually, he did understand why. He'd fallen in love with her, and how the hell he'd let that happen, he had no clue.

Except he hadn't had a choice in the matter, had he? Jordan Flynn was the most special woman he'd ever met, and it was too damned bad he couldn't give her what she wanted and needed. That he wasn't worthy of the love he'd felt from her, a love that she'd given him without condition or words. It made everything inside him hurt, but she deserved a man who could give all of himself to her. A man who wasn't missing a part of himself that was gone forever.

A hard rap on his door had him swinging toward it in surprise. Surely it wouldn't be Jordan, weeks after they'd parted. His heart beating a little harder, he got up and opened the door to see it was Bob.

"What's up?"

"We have a search and rescue situation. I know that's something you excel at, and thought you'd want to be involved for a couple reasons."

Something he excelled at. Nobody but Jordan knew how little that was true.

"A couple reasons?" He grabbed his coat and followed Bob down the hallway to the hangar. "What do you mean?"

"A woman was injured at a nearby station that doesn't have medical care, and Jordan went with Lance to look at her. Except a sudden storm blew in and they never showed."

It felt like his heart completely stopped for a long moment before it began hammering against his ribs. "Jordan? Lost in a storm?"

"Apparently. The Ski-Doos are ready to go."

He ran the rest of the way to the hangar. Threw on his coat, strapped the light to his forehead, shoved his feet into the skis and got going. Twenty-four-hour daylight didn't mean it was easy to see, not when the snow was coming down hard, and blowing nearly sideways in the wind. He and the others in the rescue team fanned out, and he squinted across the barren, icy landscape, praying he'd see her.

"Jordan! Lance! Where are you?"

Nothing. No answer. No sign. The thirty minutes since he'd started looking felt like hours, terror building in his chest that he wouldn't find her in time. In this kind of cold, hypothermia could happen fast, even with all the layers everyone wore outdoors. Being stranded meant little body heat being generated, and the thought of Jordan lying unconscious somewhere, dying a slow, frozen death, felt unbearable.

No. He would not let that happen to her. No matter what it took, he would find her and Lance.

Through the swirling snow, he thought he saw a patch of red. His heart pounded hard and his breath came fast as he punched the Ski-Doo into high gear. And then he saw it was Jordan, with Lance lying next to her. For real.

"Jordan!" He leaped off the Ski-Doo and slapped the throttle off before running to her, slipping on the ice before he dropped to his knees in front of her. Lance's eyes were open and he was conscious, but Jordan's eyelids were closed, her lashes covered with snow. He could see she was shivering, that her breathing was shallow, and his chest tightened. Classic signs of hypothermia. Then her eyes fluttered open to stare at him.

"Jordan." He quickly shot a flare into the sky, and lit another to get the attention of the other rescuers, placing it a few feet away before he reached for her hands. He pulled off her gloves to gently rub them, trying to get her circulation going. "Jordan, can you hear me?"

"What...took you so long?"

He nearly wept in relief. "Got here as soon as I could."

Her gaze moved to the flare, then back to him. "Zeke be nimble, Zeke be quick. Zeke jumped over the candlestick." The words were slurred, but damned if her blue, frozen lips didn't curve in a small smile. "See? Sometimes the nursery rhymes make...total sense."

God, how he loved this woman. Her bravery. Her spunk. Her attitude. He kept rubbing her hands and leaned close to press his cheek to her ice-cold one, trying to warm her that way, too. "Gonna get you on the sled now. We're getting you and Lance back."

He quickly checked on Lance again, who was thankfully still conscious. "Hang in there, Lance. I'll be right back. You're both going to be okay."

He lifted Jordan into his arms and prayed with everything in him that was true. As he wrapped her in a thick blanket and secured her onto the sled attached to the snow machine, he heard the roar of the other Ski-

Doos as the team spotted the ground flare. He lifted his hand to give them a sign, then pointed at Lance. They pulled up next to Lance and jumped off their Ski-Doos and Zeke took off, knowing they'd get the man the help he needed.

Getting Jordan back as fast as possible was his priority now.

Zeke paced around the room outside the hospital, frustrated that Tony Bradshaw didn't want him by Jordan's side until he felt confident she was responding well to the warming IV and heated oxygen treatment.

"You're going to wear a hole in that brand-new floor," Bob said. "Try to relax."

"Relax? She nearly died out there!"

"But she didn't. Because you found her and saved her."

"I can't take credit. You're the one who came to tell me she was missing. And someone else could easily have found them." Though he was more grateful than he could possibly say that he'd been the lucky one. Finding her there, then seeing her open her eyes and manage a smile, to even recite one of her silly nursery rhymes while lost and nearly frozen, would always be the single most gratifying thing he'd ever experience.

"But they didn't. You did. So now what?"

"What do you mean, now what?"

"Are you going to stop being an idiot, tell the woman you love her and do whatever you can to keep her?"

"I...don't know what you're talking about."

"Jordan told me you broke it off with her, though didn't say why. Look, I know you must have been through something terrible in the past, and I'm really sorry." Bob stood and walked over to rest his hand on Zeke's shoulder. "But you can't let that pain rule your life."

"I don't let it rule my life. I just know that I don't have what a woman like Jordan deserves. I can't give her what she wants. That's why I ended it. I'm not enough for her."

"I guess you going into a snowstorm, finding her and saving her life doesn't count as enough? Loving her isn't enough?" He cocked his head. "Think about how ridiculous that sounds. Don't throw away your chance to be happy with Jordan. That chance might never come again. I know she's willing to take that chance, because she's bold and brave. Are you? Or are you a coward, protecting yourself, while you claim to be protecting her instead?"

He stood stone-still, absorbing Bob's words. Was he being a coward? Was what Bob had said a truth he hadn't let himself face? Was it time for him to look the old Zeke in the eye, and become the man he wanted to be, instead of the man he believed himself to be?

"Zeke, you can come see Jordan now, if you like," Tony said, coming into the room.

"Thanks." He turned to Bob. "And thanks to you, too."

"Anytime." Bob smiled. "Now, go. You've got some making up to do."

His heart bumped wildly in his chest as he stepped next to Jordan's bed, pulling the privacy curtain around it. Her solemn eyes met his. When he saw the discoloration of her skin from being in the cold for so long, his teeth clenched and he reached to cup her cheek in his hand, unlocking his jaw so he could speak.

"You've had a rough time of it."

"Are you talking about nearly freezing to death? Or being kicked out the door by the man I'm in love with?"

He had to smile, even as her words made his chest hurt. "Which was worse?"

"About even, I think."

"What do you think about me making both of them right?"

"How are you going to do that?"

"I found you on the snow, so that one's done. Now I need to tell you I'm sorry. Sorry I hurt you, sorry I'm an idiot and sorry I didn't realize it sooner."

"What should you have realized sooner?"

"That I love you." He sat on the side of the bed and reached for her hands. "That I was being selfish by breaking it off between us, convincing myself I was doing it to protect you. That having you in my life is the best thing that ever happened to me, and when I thought you might die out there on the ice, I knew a part of me would die with you. But you didn't die. And I'm not going to let you go, ever again."

"Oh, Zeke," she whispered. "I love you, too. I never understood how you could possibly not believe in how strong and steady you are, because I know you're the kind of man who'll always be there in good times and bad. And I'll be there for you in good times and bad. If you'll let me be."

His throat closed at her words, and he had to try twice to speak. "Thank you for believing in me, and helping me believe in myself. I didn't want to let us start an affair because I was sure it wouldn't be fair to you."

"And now?"

"Now I hope our affair will happen on ice, snow, sand and surf. For the rest of our lives. If you'll say yes."

"Yes."

She reached for him, her eyes brimming with tears. He felt his threaten to do the same, and since he wasn't quite at the point where he'd want her to see that, he carefully pulled her into his arms and gently kissed her, but not for long because her poor lips were still bruised and tender from the frostbite she'd endured.

"I've been thinking about you wanting roots and that picket fence." He held her hands and knew she was worth any change he had to make in his life for her to be happy. "I'm going to ask my university to put me on the teaching schedule year-round now. I can still do marine biology research in California, and for the climatology—"

"No."

"No? What do you want, then? To move back to England? It might take some time for me to find a position there, but—"

"No, I want to find a job in Southern California where I can still travel with you to Antarctica, or wherever else your research takes you."

He stared at her, stunned. "What about those roots you never had? I'm not sure a few months a year in San Diego would qualify, especially if we have that brood of kids that's on your list of things you want in your life. And isn't the Antarctic too scary for you now?"

"Pshaw!" She waved her hand dismissively and grinned. "A near attack by a leopard seal and getting lost in a snowstorm could never dim how it feels to kiss you under the southern lights. Being with you down here has made me see that roots and a picket fence are way overrated. I grew up a gypsy, and I've finally come to see that it's in my blood, and how I want to live my

life, after all. Including the brood of kids. If that's okay with you?"

Her words made him feel so overwhelmed he couldn't do anything but nod and hold her close against him for long minutes until he could trust himself to speak again.

"You know I have issues, right? I have panic attacks. Nightmares. But I know that I finally have to deal with all that, talk to a professional about it, because you've made me see I don't have to live that way anymore. Don't want to anymore. But do you want to wait to find out how I do before we decide on forever together? If so, I understand."

"I want to help you in that journey, like you've helped me in mine. I want us to take the rest of our journeys together."

Emotion welled in his chest. "I can't think of anything better. With a close second being kissing you under the southern lights."

"So when can we do that again?"

"Not until next winter. Unless you want to travel to the north pole for our next adventure together."

"Maybe a wedding under the aurora borealis?"

"Now you're talking." He kissed her again, and knew he was the luckiest man on Earth at either pole. "It's a date."

* * * * *

Look out for the next story in the
Doctors Under the Stars duet

Reunited in the Snow
by Amalie Berlin

*And if you enjoyed this story, check out
these other great reads from
Robin Gianna*

The Family They've Longed For
Tempted by the Brooding Surgeon
The Spanish Duke's Holiday Proposal
Baby Surprise for the Doctor Prince

All available now!